URSULA K. LE GUIN

URSULA K. LE GUIN
THE LAST INTERVIEW
and OTHER CONVERSATIONS

edited and with an introduction by DAVID STREITFELD

 MELVILLE HOUSE
BROOKLYN · LONDON

CONTENTS

INTRODUCTION

DAVID STREITFELD

Many celebrated novelists are not especially keen on interviews. They have nothing to say or they've said it all before or they'd rather spend their time writing or they're afraid of giving up the hard-won secrets to their work. An interview is, at best, something to be endured.

Ursula K. Le Guin was different. She loved the push and pull of a good conversation. Her stories were laden with meaning, but she wrote without conscious intention, as a voyage of discovery—which meant that after publication she was delighted to entertain readers' conclusions about where she ended up. She liked to do interviews in front of an audience and liked to do them by mail or email so she could weigh her replies. And she did them in person in her home, sometimes improving the transcript later, sometimes not. She always had something to say.

When necessary, Le Guin could play the role of the interviewer too, always better than whoever nominally had the job. Paul Walker, doing a Q&A for the fanzine *Luna Monthly* in 1976, could not visit her at her home in Oregon, so he asked from afar what would happen if he showed up and said, "Tell me about yourself."

"Sure," Le Guin playfully responded, "I could give you a vivid description of Mrs. Le Guin (Tall, balding, full-bearded, she met me at the door with a hearty handclasp. 'Come in and help us gut the elk' she boomed). But then I could give you other descriptions equally vivid (It was at first difficult to induce Mrs. Le Guin to speak, as she hung placidly head downward from a branch of the large catalpa tree in the drawing room)."

And then, the joke made, she cut to her point: "But what is truth, as jesting Pilate remarked, and what is the good of the cult of personality, I wonder? I mean some of us are Norman Mailer, right on, but others of us are middle-aged Portland housewives. It seems to me that my public self is in my books, and my private self is and should be of real interest only to myself and family."

She maintained that distinction for more than forty years, talking publicly but not privately. It was enough.

Some writers need experience to feed the imagination, but Le Guin's experiences were all in her head. She prided herself in having as few external stimuli as possible. She told an interviewer from Poland in 1988 her ideal schedule:

> 5:30 a.m.—wake up and lie there and think.
>
> 6:15 a.m.—get up and eat breakfast (lots).
>
> 7:15 a.m.—get to work writing, writing, writing.
>
> Noon—lunch.
>
> 1:00-3:00 p.m.—reading, music.
>
> 3:00-5:00 p.m.—correspondence, maybe house cleaning.
>
> 5:00-8:00 p.m.—make dinner and eat it.
>
> After 8:00 p.m.—I tend to be very stupid and we won't talk about this.

She felt sorry for writers who have to force themselves to the typewriter. She didn't understand writer's block. "I have always liked to work," she confessed. There was nowhere else she wanted to be, and even if there was, she couldn't get there: she didn't drive. She took a sabbatical year in London, went to Australia for a convention, and visited her family's Napa Valley ranch every summer. That was about it. "I did that introversion/extroversion test once long ago, and I was just off the charts on introvert," she told *Interview* magazine in 2015. "I was slightly inhuman. It was sort of scary."

With such a passion for routine and order, the wonder is that the books were not routine as well. She could have written forty-three volumes set in the Earthsea archipelago instead of a mere six, made a bundle off them, and, given our debased age, been just as acclaimed. But she let her inspiration guide her, and it went all over the place. She wrote novels, novellas, short stories, poetry, essays, performance art, commencement speeches, how-to-write manuals, introductions, translations, criticism, children's picture books, books for young adults, the text for photography volumes, and letters to the editor. She liked blogging, even after it was no longer in vogue. She was a political activist in word and deed. She did not like Twitter.

Her first story, at age nine, was about a man who sees elves. No one else can see them, but they get him in the end. That might have been the bleakest thing she ever wrote. She spent her twenties unknown and unpublished, learning her craft, then another five years breaking into the field of science fiction with pleasant but minor works. Then bang, in her late thirties she wrote and published her first masterpieces, *A Wizard of Earthsea* and *The Left Hand of Darkness*, within months of each other. The former was issued by an obscure Berkeley press, the latter as a paperback from Ace, the big sci-fi factory, but the reputation of both quickly transcended these modest beginnings. *Left Hand* was particularly influential with other writers, showing them how they could stretch their subject matter into areas like gender, but I suspect *Wizard* molded more readers. It taught them what they owe to the world—a reversal of most fantasy, which is about what the world owes you. *Wizard* is about power and responsibility, and how the greatest enemy is often within.

In the mid-1970s, when I was a science fiction–besotted teen, *Wizard* was reissued by Bantam with a cover showing a dragon intertwined with a town and its castle, his nostrils belching smoke. Neither too cute nor too grim, that cover sold me, and I read my first Le Guin. I liked the book and appreciated its Tolkien-flavored heroic quest, but nothing more. In 2003, covering a senseless war, I took my copy to Baghdad. At night I would crouch behind the bed in my hotel room, the safest place I could find, listening to the explosions in the distance and reading. The book had changed, acquiring depths I never noticed. I learned how Ged, the young wizard who has immense gifts and is arrogant about them, was apprenticed to the mage Ogion:

> When it rained Ogion would not even say the spell that every weatherworker knows, to send the storm aside. In a land where sorcerers come thick, like Gont or the Enlades, you may see a raincloud blundering slowly from side to side and place to place as one spell shunts it on to the next, till at last it is buffeted out over the sea where it can rain in peace. But Ogion let the rain fall where it would. He found a thick fir-tree and lay down beneath it. Ged crouched among the dripping bushes wet and sullen, and wondered what was the point of having power if you were too wise to use it, and wished he had gone as prentice to that old weatherworker of the Vale, where at least he would have slept dry. He did not speak

any of his thoughts aloud. He said not a word.
His master smiled, and fell asleep in the rain.*

Wizard, its sequels, and *Left Hand* dominated discussion of Le Guin's work for decades, with the occasional addition of *The Dispossessed* for those of a more political bent. This irritated the writer, who found herself endlessly talking about books she had written long ago. When Nick Gevers, in an interview reprinted in this volume, asked her in 2001 about her current work, her relief was palpable. As she moved through her eighties, the entire scope of her career became visible and she became a cultural sage. In 2007, *Death Ray* magazine tried to sum things up:

Q: You are at the height of a very fruitful career. You've already had a huge influence on many writers and readers. What do you hope your legacy will be?

LE GUIN: Irreverence toward undeserved authority, and passionate respect for the power of the word. Oh, and my books staying in print, too.

Q: Which are your favorite books from your own work?

LE GUIN: I love them all, the flawed little bastards.

---

* Ursula K. Le Guin, *A Wizard of Earthsea*. Bantam: 1975, p. 18.

• • •

The first interview with a writer I can remember reading was a conversation with Le Guin in a science fiction fanzine called *Algol* in 1975. It was originally a radio interview, and like many of the author's interviews, she reworked it heavily for print. She had won a Hugo from the science fiction fans for *The Left Hand of Darkness*, and a National Book Award for children's literature for *The Farthest Shore*, the third Earthsea book, and so the interviewer rather crassly asked:

Q: Which would you rather have, a National Book Award or a Hugo?

LE GUIN: Oh, a Nobel, of course.

Q: They don't give Nobel Prize awards for fantasy.

LE GUIN: Maybe I can do something for peace.

By the time she was in her eighties, they were giving Nobels for fantasy (Portugal's José Saramago, for one) and she herself was a contender. I told her one year she was given odds of twenty-five to one, and she fired back that she knew what that meant: "All I have to do in the next twenty-five years is outlive the other twenty-four writers." Le Guin, in retrospect, never had a chance with the Swedish Academy, which was enmeshed in a sexual harassment and abuse scandal that it covered up for years.

Someday scholars will seek out every Le Guin interview in every fanzine and Oregon newspaper. They will transcribe all the Q&As on YouTube and track down the public appearances that are not. The result will be several fat volumes, full of wisdom and other good things. In the meantime, here's a sampling of some quotes from interviews that did not fit into this volume, but which I found particularly illuminating.

Why even her bleakest stories are interwoven with optimism:

> It may just be a refusal to take the counsel of despair. I think to admit despair and to revel in it—as many 20th- and 21st-century writers do— is an easy way out. Whenever I get really really depressed and discouraged about our politics in America and what we are doing, ecologically speaking, globally speaking, [with] our mad rush to destroy the world, it's very easy to say, "To hell with us. This species is not successful." Something tells me I have no right to say that. There are good people. Who am I to judge? The problem with despair is it gets judgmental.*

How she became a feminist in the early 1970s:

> It was a real mind shift. And I was a grown woman with kids. And mothers of children were

---

* "Getting Away with Murder," The Millions, Paul Morton, January 31, 2013. https://themillions .com/2013/01/getting-away-with-murder-the-millions-interviews-ursula-k-le-guin.html.

not welcome among a lot of early feminists. I was living the bad dream. I was a mommy. You know there's always prejudice in a revolutionary movement. I wasn't even sure I was welcome. And I wasn't to some of those people. It took a lot of thinking for me to find what kind of feminist I could be and why I wanted to be a feminist.[*]

The humor in her work that many cannot see:

I roll around laughing sometimes writing it, and then the critics come on and they are so damned serious and talk about Discourses and Epiphanies and Battles of Good and Evil and all that. I remember trying to show the scriptwriter for *Lathe of Heaven* that the book was essentially comic. His script was quite humorless. Heavy-handed. So the poor guy laboriously stuck in some bad jokes, and we had to take them out again. Humor is a chancy thing; and when it's an element of a serious book, a lot of people just miss it, perhaps because they don't expect complexity, and there isn't a laugh track.[†]

On science fiction:

---

[*]   "My Last Conversation with Ursula K. Le Guin," Literary Hub, John Freeman, January 24, 2018. https://lithub.com/my-last-conversation-with-ursula-k-le-guin/.

[†]   "2001 Book Awards". Pacific Northwest Bookseller Association. Archived from the original on June 21, 2013. Interview by Cindy Heidemann. https://web.archive.org/web/20130621065514/http://www.pnba.org/2001BookAwards.html

Here we've got science fiction, the most flexible, adaptable broad range, imaginative, crazy form that prose fiction has ever attained and we're going to let it be used for making toy plastic ray guns that break when you play with them and prepackaged, precooked, predigested, indigestible flavorless TV dinners and big inflated rubber balloons containing nothing but hot air? Well, I say the hell with that.*

On the unconventional form of her far-future Napa Valley novel *Always Coming Home*, which reversed her usual method of composition:

You know, a novelist's job is largely leaving things out. Getting the story flowing clear of all the junk around it—the river banks. Well, in this book, I wanted to include the river banks. Not only the river, but the banks of the river and the bed of the river and the trees over the river. So in some ways I had to unlearn everything I'd learned about writing a book . . . Stuff has to go down inside of you, get into the dark and turn into something else, before you can use it in art. If you use raw experience, straight experience, you're doing journalism which is another discipline.†

---

* *On the Media,* hosted by Bob Garfield and Brooke Gladstone and produced by WNYC; broadcast by WNYC; January 26, 2018.

† Irv Broughton, *The Writer's Mind: Interviews With American Authors*, Vol. 2 (University of Arkansas Press, 1990).

Sex in fiction:

> I find that as I get older, I write more freely and
> with more pleasure about sexuality. I don't write
> very much about sex, the act of sex itself, because
> I don't like to read about it. I have never enjoyed
> reading about sex. It's like reading about a foot-
> ball game or a wrestling match. It might be fun to
> watch or to do but it isn't any fun to read about.[*]

On form:

> I don't feel the short story is a tight form. It can
> be made so; tight plotters and gimmick-ending
> writers like it so. But in itself it is potentially im-
> mense. To have read Chekhov is to know that as
> a certainty. It's like the sonnet. Fourteen lines
> and a demanding rhyme scheme seems to be a
> tight, closed form, but Wordsworth got all of
> London and all the sunrise into it.[†]

Whether she saw herself as a radical:

> Yeah, I do. That's easy enough. Of course, being a
> radical in the United States . . . you can be slightly

---

[*] Helene Escudie, *Entretein avec Ursula K. Le Guin*, in "Conversations With Ursula K. Le
Guin," edited by Carl Freedman (University Press of Mississippi, 2008).

[†] "An Interview with Ursula K. Le Guin," Association of Writers & Writing Programs,
Ramola D, October/November 2003. https://www.awpwriter.org/magazine_media
/writers_chronicle_view/2293/an_interview_with_ursula_k._le_guin.

left of center and you're immediately called "radical."
I've always been something of a socialist in politics
and so on, and that's extremely radical over here. I
think some of my writing is radical in a sort of quiet
way. I don't go in for dangerous writing and shock-
ing people and so on. If radical means getting down
to the roots of things you write, then I do see that as
my job, trying to get down to the roots.[*]

Why the map of Earthsea came before the stories:

At first the map could be adjusted to fit the story.
This is the beauty of fantasy—your invention al-
ters at need, at least at first. If I didn't want it to
take two weeks, say, to get from one island to
another, I could simply move the islands closer.
But once you've decided that the islands are that
far apart, that's it. The map is drawn. You have to
adjust to it as if it were a reality. And it is.[†]

How being a Westerner influenced her work and career:

Being far from the centers of commercial publishing and the ingroups and the anxieties and
influences of East Coast literary circles, where

---

[*] "Ursula Le Guin talks Sci-fi Snobbery, Adaptations, & Troublemaking," *Den of Geek*,
   Louisa Mellor, April 7, 2015. https://www.denofgeek.com/us/books-comics/ursula-le
   -guin/245224/ursula-le-guin-talks-sci-fi-snobbery-adaptations-troublemaking.

[†] Larry McCaffery and Sinda Gregory, *Alive and Writing: Interviews With American Authors of the 1980s* (University of Illinois Press, 1987).

the big question is, Am I with it?—we left-edgers, boondockers, prairie chickens, etc., often have an attitude which is more describable as, Oh, the hell with it. This is healthy. I don't think it's ever really healthy for a writer to be an insider.[*]

The reality of made-up things:

It has something to do with the very nature of fiction. That age-old question, Why don't I just write about what's real? A lot of 20th century—and 21st century—American readers think that that's all they want. They want nonfiction. They'll say, I don't read fiction because it isn't real. This is incredibly naive. Fiction is something that only human beings do, and only in certain circumstances. We don't know exactly for what purposes. But one of the things it does is lead you to recognize what you did not know before.

This is what a lot of mystical disciplines are after—simply seeing, really seeing, really being aware. Which means you're recognizing the things around you more deeply, but they also seem new. So the seeing-as-new and recognition are really the same thing.[†]

---

[*]   "An Interview with Ursula K. Le Guin," AWP, Ramona D, October/November 2003.

[†]   "Ursula K. Le Guin, The Art of Fiction No. 221," *The Paris Review*, John Wray, Fall 2013, Issue 206. https://www.theparisreview.org/interviews/6253/ursula-k-le-guin-the-art-of-fiction-no-221-ursula-k-le-guin.

Learning to argue with Tolstoy:

> **Q:** You said you used to be too respectful to disagree
> with Tolstoy but after you got into your sixties your
> faculty of respect atrophied and you began to ask
> rude questions of Tolstoy. What were they?
>
> **LE GUIN:** "Why did you say 'all happy families
> are alike'?" You know, the famous beginning
> of Anna Karenina. What a ridiculous thing to
> say. Show me two happy families that are alike.
> Show me two happy families.
>
> **Q:** That'd be a good start, to find them and com-
> pare them!
>
> **LE GUIN:** Right, yes. There are families that are
> happy from time to time, I grew up in one. But
> the idea of them being "a happy family" or a fam-
> ily that is continuously happy . . . what are you
> talking about, Tolstoy? I think he got a good first
> sentence, it sounded good, he couldn't let it go.*

How our uncertain reality requires new storytellers:

> One of the American science-fiction writers I ad-
> mire most is Philip K. Dick, and Philip K. Dick's

---

* *The Book Show*, hosted by Ramona Koval and produced by the Australian Broadcasting
Commission; broadcast by ABC Radio National; May 4, 2008.

world involves immense tracts of pure insanity. It's a world which is always in danger of falling to pieces. It is an accurate picture of what is going on in a lot of people's heads and how the world actually does affect us—this weird, disjointed, unexpected world we're living in now. Well now, Phil Dick reflects that by using a sane, matter-of-fact prose to describe the completely insane things that happen in his novels. It is a way of mirroring reality.[*]

As she grew older, she became even more irreverent. Here, a year before her death, she takes on a question from the *Times Literary Supplement*, "What will your field look like 25 years from now?":

My field? What is my field, I wonder. My favorite field is the one below the barn at the old ranch in California. I hope in twenty-five years it looks just the way it does now, all wild oats and chicory and foxtail and voles and jackrabbits and quail.[†]

Life is a journey back to where you started from, Le Guin always said. True voyage is return. When you get there, you might know a little more than when you began.

---

[*] Irv Broughton, *The Writer's Mind: Interviews With American Authors*, Vol. 2 (University of Arkansas Press, 1990).

[†] "Twenty Questions with Ursula K. Le Guin," *The Times Literary Supplement*, March 4, 2017. https://www.the-tls.co.uk/articles/public/twenty-questions-ursula-le-guin/.

Isn't the real question this: Is the work worth doing? Am I, a human being, working for what I really need and want—or for what the State or the
advertisers tell me I want? Do I choose? I think
that's what anarchism comes down to. Do I let
my choices be made for me, and so go along with
the power game, or do I choose, and accept the
responsibility for my choice? In other words, am
I going to be a machine-part, or a human being?*

• • •

I'm reading *A Wizard of Earthsea* again, this time aloud,
to my nine-year-old daughter. I still have the same well-
traveled copy of the book I bought in 1975, although it is
beginning to disintegrate. We've made it to the part where
Ged, whose arrogance has caused him to let loose a mon-
strous shadow creature on the world, is sailing to confront
the dragon. Lily wants to know why Ged has to fight the
dragon instead of making friends with it, and why all
the wizards are men. I tell her Le Guin eventually had
the same questions, and that the sequels show a different
picture of life in Earthsea.

The book has shifted for me again. As a teenager I saw
it as a heroic adventure tale. During my brief stint as a war
correspondent it was a parable of power. Now it is a book
about reckoning with oneself, about how to live fully and

---

* Jonathan Ward, "Interview with Ursula K. Le Guin," *Algol* No. 24, May 1975.

honestly. Ged's only hope for survival is to turn the tables on his shadowy pursuer, to hunt the hunter, to take back the world. It is a message that seems particularly potent at this troubled moment in our country, one that Le Guin echoed in her 2014 National Book Foundation lifetime achievement acceptance speech:

"We live in capitalism, its power seems inescapable— but then, so did the divine right of kings. Any human power can be resisted and changed by human beings. Resistance and change often begin in art. Very often in our art, the art of words."

THE GIFT OF PLACE

INTERVIEW BY THE 10 POINT 5 EDITORIAL COLLECTIVE
10 POINT 5 MAGAZINE
SPRING 1977

Interview conducted by Karen McPherson, Peter Jensen, Alison Halderman, David Zeltzer, and Karen Kramer

PETER JENSEN: You write science fiction. Do you have any particular vision of the future?

URSULA K. LE GUIN: The thing about science fiction is, it isn't really about the future. It's about the present. But the future gives us great freedom of imagination. It's like a mirror. You can see the back of your own head.

KAREN MCPHERSON: You've said that writing science fiction is sometimes like performing "thought experiments." You establish a set of conditions and then see where they lead. For instance, in *The Dispossessed* you set up the conditions of an anarchist society, almost as though you're working in a laboratory. Can you actually learn about anarchism from this—whether and how it could work? Its strengths and problems?

LE GUIN: Sure. Calling it a "thought experiment" is maybe a little scientific, clinical. When I said that, I was grasping at respectability. But it is a process, a technique. I used it

fairly consciously in *The Left Hand of Darkness*. I wanted
to see what would happen in an androgynous society. *The
Dispossessed* was less experimental. I went into it thinking I knew where it would lead. But in *The Left Hand of
Darkness* I kept getting stuck, because although I'd worked
hard trying to plan out that world, I wasn't sure how an
androgynous person would think. And I would wonder:
What would Estraven's reactions be here? So I'd sit back
and say all right, I won't plan what I'm going to write next,
and quite often one of those myths would come out. I can
only interpret it by saying it was my unconscious instruct-
ing me as to how androgynes think. Anyway, whenever I'd
written one of those myths I would put it aside and go on,
and I would have gotten over this hump or this knot in
the story. I didn't intend to include them. They were just
my problem-solving devices, but then when the book was
done, and I looked at them, I thought, Well gee, some of
them are kind of nice in themselves, and they might help
other people read the book, so I did put most of them in. I
was so deeply into that world while I was writing that book
that I could even write in Karhidish. I could write poetry
in Karhidish.

ALISON HALDERMAN: How did you conceive of the landscape in Earthsea?

LE GUIN: That's a big question. You're kind of getting at
what fantasy creation is. I cannot say I invented it. That's
not what it feels like. It feels like discovering it. You've got

this place inside yourself which is an ocean with a lot of is-lands in it. Islands with these peculiar people. And you find out about them as you write about them. It is certainly re-lated to dreaming, or to deliberate fantasy in the psycholo-gist's sense. Not daydreaming, which is just wandering. But it's a very odd business, and I can't explain it.

MCPHERSON: You write a lot about dreams and reality in *The Word for World Is Forest*.

LE GUIN: Yes. The weird thing is after I wrote it Charles Tart sent me his book called *Altered States of Consciousness* and asked me if I knew anything about the Senoi tribe in Malaysia. An anthropologist in the 1930s went in and studied them—their culture was based on dreaming. But no one seems to have found them since, and I wonder if he dreamed them up. The Senoi use dreaming—they cul-tivate it. They are so close to my little green men! There are no tales of murder in that tribe. Their neighbors were warlike tribes but nobody would attack the Senoi because they were said to be magicians and sorcerers, although in fact they did not use magic—they used dreams. When they met at the breakfast table with their children, a little kid might say, "I dreamed that I fell," and they'd answer, "How neat! Where did you fall and what did you see?" If he didn't know where he fell to, he'd go back the next night and *dream* where he fell to. Or for instance if you meet a tiger in your dream there are all kinds of things you can do. You can let it eat you and see what that's like, or you can eat the tiger. Or make friends with it. Jung wrote about the same sort of thing. When you meet a character in a dream, and you go back the next day and find out what he wanted. When I was trying to bring up my kids, the idea was never to take a dream seriously. You were supposed to tell your kid, "Oh, that was just a dream." That never felt right to me. I never did it.

DAVID ZELTZER: You really got into the substance of dreams in *The Lathe of Heaven*.

LE GUIN: Yes, I wrote that in the sixties, right in the middle of all the sleep and dream research. They seem to have hit a plateau with that stuff now but back then it was a hot topic. I read all I could of the current research and the book just grew out of it. I've studied Jung just recently. He was a real shaman. He had great mana and power. It comes out through his books. I am under his influence for a week after reading one of his books; you have to be on your guard a bit, with a personality that strong. I had to start reading Jung: after I wrote the Earthsea trilogy, people would come up to me and say, "Of course, the Shadow is straight from Jung." And I said, "The *what* from *who*?" Jung has been criticized for being too religious, too mystical. Actually, I think he's no more religious than Taoism . . . I find Jung very useful. As a woman and an artist. And as a middle-aged person. Jung never discounted Freud. He just felt Freud placed too much importance on some things, like the Oedipus complex. Jung was interested in middle-aged people heading downslope after the Freudian battles of the twenties and thirties. By the time you're thirty-five or older, you have it all, but then you have to put it all together. When you know how to do your work. I'm fascinated with the idea of the integrated person. Another fascinating thing is that I don't think I could have written Earthsea if I'd read Jung first. But it's completely "from" Jung. I can be reading along now and say, "Oh, is *that* what I was doing?" So my writing was almost like a proof of Jung's theories.

ZELTZER: I notice there's no anima in your books.

LE GUIN: Of course not—I'm a woman. But the animus writes my books. My animus, what inspires me, is definitely male. People talk about muses—well, my muse ain't no girl in a filmy dress, that's for sure. But of course this is all metaphor.*

MCPHERSON: In Earthsea there was the beginning of an anima figure in Arha except Ged didn't follow her—he set her aside and pursued his own destiny.

LE GUIN: Yes. Ged shouldn't connect. Sometimes I have no control over these things. Wizards usually have to be celibate or even virgin. I don't know why. But when you draw on the unconscious as much as I do, you should trust it.

MCPHERSON: I wonder, though, whether some of the

---

* The anima is the unconscious feminine side of a man; the animus is the unconscious masculine side of a woman.

archetypes we accept are formed by stereotypes that we have to learn to break out of. Rulag, in *The Dispossessed*, was a similar character to Ged, unconnected and unconnectable, setting aside family ties to pursue her own destiny. But Ged's actions seem natural; Rulag's bother us, seem somehow unnatural.

LE GUIN: Yes, though I think if I had a witch in Earthsea she would have been like Ged, or probably *more* independent. But thank God for feminism. We are learning to separate the stereotypes from the genuine archetype.

MCPHERSON: I know you're always hearing comments and questions about the fact that you write from men's point of view in nearly all your books. But it strikes me that you come up with a lot of powerful women this way, perhaps more diverse than the men you create. In *The Dispossessed* there are three very vital women, Rulag and Takver and, indirectly, Odo. Each one seems to deal with a different part of what women are about, but all of them have something important to say about women's liberation.

LE GUIN: I try to deal with women that way. I'm a woman, so naturally I write as a woman. I can't help doing that. And the women I write about tend to be more varied, more complicated; the men are more conventional. I recently received a manuscript from Suzy McKee Charnas. She's written a very good book, but she's having trouble selling it because it has no men in it, and the publishers say, "No one will buy this; it's just all women." Suzy has set me thinking about this a whole lot. She says that it's much harder to write from the point of view of women, because we write—in part—from all that we've *read*. There's no tradition for us to follow. Most of the books about women were written by men. Who else do we have? George Eliot, the Brontës, Jane Austen, Virginia Woolf. So we take the easy way and take a man as the main character, and then have women around him who are strong, but sort of hidden, side characters.

JENSEN: There seem to be only two conventions in science fiction for men. They can be either soldiers or diplomats.

LE GUIN: Yes, well, we don't have conventions either for new women or new men. This is something we have to work out of.

JENSEN: Or anthropologists. That's a third alternative. Like Lyubov in *The Word for World Is Forest*. You use that alternative.

LE GUIN: That's the kind of man I knew. These are the people I grew up with. They were always around the house—anthropologists and Indians. And they were fine people. Many of them were refugees from Germany. And then they were ethnologists as well, doing fieldwork: Twice displaced. And so they didn't fit the conventional roles.

MCPHERSON: You talk about the lack of available models in literature to break the conventional roles. What about some of the contemporary women writers: Atwood, Lessing?

LE GUIN: I don't read many contemporary novels. I tend to wait a while . . . Margaret Drabble is one contemporary woman novelist I really like. Doris Lessing drives me up a wall. I read *Briefing for a Descent Into Hell*, and the first fifty pages were just great, but then she cops out. She really blows it. I wanted to throw the book across the room!

MCPHERSON: I wouldn't judge Lessing on the basis of that book. But some of the others—like the Children of Violence series—*The Four-Gated City* is really science fiction.

LE GUIN: And her newest one [*Memoirs of a Survivor*] is too, isn't it? But she's avoided the science fiction label. By writing straight fiction *first*.

KAREN KRAMER: Do you ever think that label limits your audience? Do you ever resent it?

LE GUIN: It does limit the audience, of course. And some science fiction writers are very angry about that. But that's changing too. More people are overlooking the labels. And it's essentially a marketplace thing. It's a publisher's convenience—if they stick that label on it, it's a sure sale, if you want to know the filthy truth. That is why such a label means nothing anymore. I feel very free in science fiction, probably more free to write with the label than without, though I think of myself simply as a novelist. But if I had to write for money, and it were up to me—I might *demand* the science fiction label. The point is to get the books out and read, isn't it?

JENSEN: In the Soviet Union, [dissident writers Andrei] Sinyavsky and [Yuli] Daniel have said that it's common to use science fiction as a cover for social satire.

LE GUIN: Yes, but the Soviet government has caught on to that. The Strugatsky brothers are really good writers. They write science fiction and they even use the U.S. or Canada instead of Russia, in order to disguise it one step further, but it's obvious social satire; and they are being shut up now. Their manuscripts are not being approved. Here we don't need those covers, but science fiction is a natural medium for social satire.

JENSEN: I just finished reading *The Word for World Is Forest*. I'm coming from an anti-war background. Did this book come from your other works, a composite, or was it based on something you were told about Vietnam?

LE GUIN: I wrote that in 1968 in England when things were getting hotter and hotter in Vietnam. I was always in the peace movement in Portland. Not that it was much of anything, but at least we went down and walked around once or twice a year. In England there were peace marches, but it was different for an American. My hands were sort of tied. I felt trapped, so it came out in that story, I guess. It's the most topical story I ever wrote, the pain and outrage that wouldn't be put down.

JENSEN: You write about anarchism in *The Dispossessed*. Are you in touch with any international anarchist movements?

LE GUIN: I've received magazines from a lot of anarchist groups since I wrote *The Dispossessed*. London is full of anarchists, so is New York, and the Southwest. But I guess it's inherently impossible to organize anarchists, isn't it? And it's discouraging, because all these groups seem to be falling apart with internal dissension. Perhaps the anarchists have gotten so defensive, being a small, essentially unorganized movement, that they end up getting defensive with each other, among themselves.

KRAMER: Some people criticize science fiction as being too fatalistic.

LE GUIN: There's a trend in a lot of science fiction to be extrapolative—the doomsday visions. This kind of work is very depressing. It doesn't open up the future. Some of it has been very powerful. John Brunner is a doomsday writer. He's a moral, concerned man. He says that what he's saying is, "Don't go this way!" Books like that are stop signs. But people do get tired of being faced with that again and again.

ZELTZER: How much do you draw on fairy tales or myths?

LE GUIN: Well, it's useless to differentiate them; you always end up with the same damn archetypes . . . Someone told me once there are only five themes for science fiction.

MCPHERSON: What are they?

LE GUIN: He didn't say. One was the "first contact" story, of course.

HALDERMAN: Don't people tend to choose an archetype they like and then seek out books that use that theme?

LE GUIN: Sure. Because people always need new symbols and metaphors.

ZELTZER: You use the idea of time displacement in a lot of your books, where people travel through outer space at less than light speed and then come back to find that in their short time in space their home planet has aged a few hundred years.

LE GUIN: Yes, and this is a very old theme in fairy tales: going under the hill with the fairies overnight, coming back in the village and it's been a hundred years.

HALDERMAN: Science fiction likes to take traditional old fairy tales and magic and to explain them in a scientific context.

LE GUIN: I don't like that at all. Things like *Chariots of the*

Gods? really put me off. It's not a real explanation. It seems to destroy the magic when people try to give scientific rationalizations. That's different from taking an old myth and dressing it up in new metaphors.*

ZELTZER: A lot of science fiction seems to equate new metaphors with new technology. You're much more of a humanist.

LE GUIN: I've never seen why science fiction can't have people in it. Unless all you want is a wiring-diagram type of story. But I don't write those. And they very soon get boring, unless you're sixteen years old. There's got to be SF written for grownups. And that means making the characters recognizably human.

ZELTZER: In The *Wizard of Earthsea*, did you know what that thing was going to be—the thing that attacked Ged?

LE GUIN: No, I didn't. I mean, of course I had some idea. You have to have a feeling of the shape of a book before you begin it. But I didn't know what the thing was going to be. After I finished the book, people would tell me: "Oh, I knew *right away* what it was!" This really annoyed me, because *I* didn't. I didn't know until just sometime before Ged did.

And do you want to know where that thing came from?

---

* Erich von Daniken's *Chariots of the Gods? Unsolved Mysteries of the Past* was a huge bestseller in the early 1970s. It posited that ancient civilizations had been helped along by alien visitors.

I had gotten a microscope about six years ago to look at animals in drops of water. I put a drop of water from some moss on the slide and got it into focus and there it was! It looked like a furry bear with six legs but no face. It looked very large under the microscope—a monster. There it was, staring up at me, with no face. It was terrifying. Have you ever felt that? I looked it up later and found out what it was—they're called water bears. Eight or ten cells, I think.

ZELTZER: You write scary scenes well. That one in *Planet of Exile* about the snowghoul was really effective.

LE GUIN: That's a nice compliment. I've never been able to do villains very well so I guess I do monsters. I haven't had too many villains.

JENSEN: Davidson, in *The Word for World is Forest*, was a villain.

LE GUIN: Yes, Captain Davidson is my only real villain. I don't know why I can't write villains. I enjoy them in other people's books. Dickens has the best villains.

ZELTZER: The wizard Cob, at the end of the Earthsea trilogy, the one that was pulling the plug on the world . . . ?

LE GUIN: The wizard that went wrong. But you don't see very much of him. He wasn't really developed as a villain.

JENSEN: It didn't take Ged much to overcome him.

LE GUIN: It took Ged everything. He had to give up all his power.

MCPHERSON: One of your major themes seems to be distinguishing truth from lies—the idea that there exists some basic, unassailable truth.

JENSEN: There's a Vietnamese saying that it's impossible to lie in poetry . . .

LE GUIN: That's a nice one. Well, you're not supposed to be able to lie in mindspeech—this appears in many of my books—how can you lie when you're communicating directly mind to mind? And in the Earthsea books the old language which the dragons speak is the language in which things have their true names. This is the source of the magic and power of the wizards of Earthsea. They learn the true names. This is where Ged derived his power.

ZELTZER: In *The Left Hand of Darkness* you use another psycho-spiritual concept. How did you come up with the business of foretelling the future in that book?

LE GUIN: The means I gave the foretellers for foretelling the future actually came from reading some stuff about schizophrenia. Some people think that schizophrenics may be slightly displaced in time, which is perhaps a little mystical for most psychologists to swallow, but it seems to work sometimes. And so I threw in a couple of schizophrenics among the foretellers and tried to play with that idea. Philip K. Dick plays with it, you know, in a marvelous book called *Martian Time-Slip*. And if you want to know—I hope you don't know—what it's like to be mad from inside, read that book. Because he knows, and he puts it down, and he brings you out the other side. I think he's one of our best SF writers, and one of the best American novelists.

HALDERMAN: What do you think of Harlan Ellison?

LE GUIN: Harlan is very strong meat, and if you like it, of course you love it. Harlan is a volcano in perpetual eruption, and if you can take a lot of lava in the face, if you don't mind that, it's tremendous. If you get a little singed sometimes you have to draw back now and then.

HALDERMAN: Have you ever been approached about making a movie from any of your books?

LE GUIN: Oh yeah, everybody's approached about movie rights, and then they go away again. I personally don't think my books are film stuff. Except I have a dream. If you have read my book *The Lathe of Heaven*, I would like to see Mel Brooks make a movie out of it. With Gene Wilder as George. Gene Wilder *is* George.

MCPHERSON: *The Lathe of Heaven* is a very funny book.

LE GUIN: I've been locked into an image of being either depressing or extremely moral, and that's boring. *The Lathe of Heaven* was the first funny book I wrote and the most despairing. I think a lot of writers take refuge in humor when it's something that is pretty horrible or that they're scared of. And humor is a marvelous defense, isn't it? Well, look at dirty jokes; everybody's kind of scared of sex one way or another so we all tell dirty jokes and laugh at them wildly.

MCPHERSON: When did you first get a sense of yourself as a writer?

LE GUIN: I always wrote. And I was so arrogant. I didn't even say I wanted to be a writer. I thought to myself: I am a writer. I took a creative writing course in college. It was taught by a man who wrote for *The Saturday Evening Post* under a feminine pen name. I decided I was allergic to creative writing at that point. Writing my books has had nothing to do with any teaching. I qualified myself to earn a living otherwise, because I knew I wouldn't do it with my books. And I just wrote and sent it out to editors and got it back again. For about ten years. I hate to tell people that. It sounds so discouraging.

KRAMER: Do you ever sit down to write and nothing comes?

LE GUIN: Yeah, it's a disease all writers have, and it's called writer's block. The longest period I have had it, so far, was over two years. And it's miserable.

MCPHERSON: Once you're into a major work, like a novel, that has to be written over an extended period of time, how do you maintain the creative flow and deal with the constant interruptions?

LE GUIN: Hemingway, I think it was, had a definite and useful word of advice here. When you stop in the middle of a story or a novel, he said, never stop at a stopping place; go past it a little or stop short of it. Stop even in the middle of a sentence. Tomorrow when you come back to it you can read back the last few paragraphs, or pages, until you come to the "oh yeah, this is what happened next" and you can hook back up into your unconscious flow. That starting and stopping is sometimes a very hairy business.

MCPHERSON: How about the problem of never seeming to finish anything?

LE GUIN: This happens to young writers in particular (though I hate to use terms like "younger writers"), but the real trouble again may be getting started. It's not that you don't have an idea. But you write the beginning and then you go back and rewrite the beginning, and you never got off page one. It's kind of a syndrome, and I have a rash piece of advice which is—Go on, page two, page three, and *never* *look back*. Get *something* finished, no matter how lousy it is. *Then* take it and tear it to pieces and squeeze it till the blood runs and rewrite it fifty times. But I think what you've got is perfectionism trouble, and perfectionists cannot get going unless they kind of do violence to their own instincts, and just blast ahead.

MCPHERSON: But I suppose the other danger is that you will write two hundred pages of something and then have to admit that it won't work, that you're going to have to trash it completely.

LE GUIN: I'm much more that kind of writer. I do many, many false starts. In fact, everything I wrote before I was twenty-nine is like that. I keep it in boxes. That's what big empty attics are good for. But it was all learning. I was a late bloomer. There were at least four novels in those early years. They were probably the worst novels that have ever been written.

JENSEN: How can you tell when a book you're writing is finished?

LE GUIN: Well, it varies . . . it's just like making a pot on a wheel, which I can't do by the way, but I've watched other people do it—there comes a point when the pot is done, and you'd better take your hands off it. You've got the shape you want. Now with a pot it's lovely, because it's all there at once. The writing of a book takes place in time. But it really is the same thing. There comes a point when it's done. You've got to know when to stop. Which means that before you start you've got to have some vague general idea about what that shape is.

JENSEN: Do you usually let people in your stories write the story for you?

LE GUIN: Sometimes. Sometimes it doesn't happen at all. Sometimes I feel myself in control of them, manipulating them. But characters do take over. Most novelists talk about this phenomenon, with a little awe. It is a little scary, when you've got a character and you can't shut him up.

JENSEN: Do you just allow that to happen?

LE GUIN: Up to a point. The character I've written that gave me the most trouble is the wizard Ged, in the Earthsea books. He is completely autonomous. And in [*The Farthest Shore*] I had to do an awful lot of revising, cutting out stuff that Ged was telling *me* but that everybody would have gotten real bored reading.

ZELTZER: You use a lot of dialogue.

LE GUIN: I think I am not very good at dialogue and therefore I work on it as hard as I can. I don't have the real ear for dialogue, which is probably just a gift from God. I would say my gift is the gift of place. I'm extremely place-conscious. For instance, when I am homesick, I don't really think of the people, I think of the rooms that those people are in. I want to be in that room—it kind of implies the people that belong in that room. But this seems to be how my imagination works. And so I *am* good at that.

HALDERMAN: You do invent wonderful landscapes. The Earthsea trilogy creates such a vivid picture of the sea—have you done a lot of sailing?

LE GUIN: All that sailing is complete fakery. It's amazing what you can fake. I've never sailed anything in my life except a nine-foot catboat, and that was in the Berkeley basin in about three feet of water. And we managed to sink it. The sail got wet and it went down while we sang "Nearer My God to Thee." We had to wade to shore, and go back to the place we'd rented it and tell them. They couldn't believe it. "You did *what*?" You know, it's interesting, they always tell people to write about what they know about. But you don't have to know about things, you just have to be able to imagine them really well.

KRAMER: Do you read a lot of science?

LE GUIN: I don't have a head for math so I can't get very far. I wanted to be a biologist when I was a kid, but I got stuck on the math; I've got one of those blockheads. But I read the works for peasants, and I follow what interests me.

MCPHERSON: What about all that physics in *The Dispossessed*?

LE GUIN: I had to get very deeply into that—using mainly [J. T.] Fraser's *The Voices of Time*, have you heard of it? It's a sort of general compilation of works about time. There hasn't been a whole lot written about time that a peasant can understand. I didn't show *The Dispossessed* to any scientists before it was printed, but later I took it to a friend at Portland State, a physicist, and he read it. He told me, "Your prediction is not too unlikely" and he said it was good gobbledygook though maybe I'd squeezed quantum mechanics a bit out of shape. It's funny, I understood what I was writing back then. It was incredible, holding it all in that precarious balance in my mind. I don't think I could follow it all now.

ZELTZER: Do you write science fiction because this is the kind of fiction you like to read?

LE GUIN: Sure. Writers are often asked, "Why do you write?" which is, you know, an impossible question. But a lot of them give that very answer. I wrote it because nobody else would, and I wanted to read it. Tolkien, as a matter of fact, said that—he said, "I knew nobody else could write it, because nobody else knew about Middle Earth."

MCPHERSON: I guess if you take that approach you're a lot less likely to end up boring your readers. You really have an extraordinary versatility—you don't seem to get stuck with one story or one theme or one character type.

LE GUIN: I hate to repeat myself. If I start repeating myself I hope I just have the guts to stop.

JENSEN: Would you say there's any kind of statement you're making in the things which you write?

LE GUIN: Of course, I suppose in everything I write I am making some sort of statement, but I don't know just what the statement is. Which I can't say I feel guilty about. If you can say exactly what you meant by a story, then why not just say it in so many words? Why go to all the fuss and feathers of making up a plot and characters? You say it that way, because it's the only way you can say it.

KRAMER: Can you tell us anything about your new book?

LE GUIN: It isn't out yet. You'll be interested, the main character is a woman. Talk about characters taking over your book . . . It's short and humble. Only 40,000 words. It takes place on a prison planet with two exiled communities. First a shipload of hard-core criminals had been dropped off there, and fifty years later a group of pacifists. It'll be called *Outcasts*, or maybe *Ringtrees* or—does anybody know a good title? *War and Peace*, maybe?*

---

* The novel was published as *The Eye of the Heron*.

NAMING MAGIC

INTERVIEW BY DOROTHY GILBERT
THE CALIFORNIA QUARTERLY, NO. 13-14
SPRING/SUMMER 1978

This interview took place in December 1976 in the house on Arch Street in North Berkeley where Ursula Le Guin's parents lived when she was born, and where she herself grew up. Ms. Le Guin met me at the door and led me through the living room and through the kitchen, where her mother looked up from some culinary project to greet us; Ms. Le Guin and I went into a small, sunlit room off the back garden, which had been her father's study. It is now her room when she comes to Berkeley to visit. Through the windows one can look out at the garden and hear the sound of a small fountain. It is a room that suggests concentration, relaxation and practical comfort; it is decorated in blacks and browns, and contains a bunk bed, several comfortable chairs and a large table. Ursula K. Le Guin is a tall, slender woman with a neat cap of straight dark hair and large dark eyes. She speaks in a deep, low, musical voice with many inflections; it is a voice that conveys humor, or delight in small ironies, particularly well. As we talked, she smoked a briar pipe.

DOROTHY GILBERT: You grew up in this house. Does it have strong associations for you of your development as a writer, of when you first developed a sense of yourself as a writer?

URSULA K. LE GUIN: Well, sure. It's a pretty strong-minded house.

GILBERT: Yes, I can see that.

LE GUIN: And a very livable house. Of course I lived here until I was seventeen, and didn't move around. So, my whole beginnings are here. And in the Napa Valley.

GILBERT: Oh, yes, there was the family home called Kishamish, in the Napa Valley. The name came from a mythical figure that your brother made up, I gather.

LE GUIN: Yes. Sort of a legend.

GILBERT: Was there much of that kind of legend-making, of make-believe, among you and your brothers in your childhood?

LE GUIN: Well—yes. All my brothers were nutty in different ways. We were all nutty. That brother is the only one who made up myths.

GILBERT: You didn't do that?

LE GUIN: Well, not in public. He told his aloud.

GILBERT: I see. Have you always assumed that you would be a writer?

LE GUIN: Yes.

GILBERT: You didn't decide one day, "That's what I'm going to do?"

LE GUIN: No, I just knew it.

GILBERT: What led you to science fiction?

LE GUIN: Trying to get published. The stuff I wrote has always been—it's had what you'd have to call a fantasy element.

GILBERT: It always did?

LE GUIN: Always, right from the start, except for the poetry. It took place in an imaginary country or something like that, and the publishers didn't know what to call it; they didn't know what it was. And they didn't publish it. And I got back to reading science fiction in my late twenties, and I thought hey, you know, maybe I could *call* my stuff science fiction. So I sent a story to Cele Lalli at *Fantastic* magazine, and she bought it. And from then on I was a science fiction writer. They found a label for me. I had a pigeonhole. You have to have a pigeonhole. You have to *start* with a pigeonhole.

GILBERT: And you can't be half in each of two pigeonholes, either!

LE GUIN: Well, you can once you get started, yes. I'm a juvenile writer, a science fiction writer, and now I'm—well, *The Dispossessed* and the Orsinian tales and so on are not labeled science fiction. Now I'm a writer. But you have to get started, apparently, in a box, with a label. Then you can break out of the box.

GILBERT: I know from speaking to other science fiction writers, like Joanna Russ, that sometimes you have frustrations if you're starting out in your career, and you try two things at once. Or if you do something that doesn't quite fit in one category or another. Then you didn't call your science fiction "science fiction" yourself.

LE GUIN: No, it really is a publisher's label, and a bookseller's label. And it's a useful label, I don't resent it. I like to go to a bookstore and find the science fiction all together. And yet in a way it has—I don't use the label much for my own stuff, partly because everybody uses it differently. It's a convenience label, but it doesn't really mean anything, and of course nobody's ever been able to define it. "What is the difference between science fiction and fantasy?" [*Laughs*]

GILBERT: Oh, yes. Of course, there's the convenient label "speculative fiction." "Spec fic."

LE GUIN: "Spec fic." Yes. [*Laughs*] It beats "sci-fic." I don't mind "s-f," but "sci-fi," for some reason, *grates*.

GILBERT: You take an obvious pleasure in dealing with myths, folk myths and magic; some of my favorite examples of that are from *A Wizard of Earthsea*, where one can follow the apprenticeship and the difficult and dangerous career of the mage Ged, and also in your story "The Word of Unbinding," where the magician keeps trying to escape, and trying to change himself into various things. I think, by the way, that you have a good deal of sophisticated fun with stereotypes—folk expectations of a sort—in your story "Vaster Than Empires and More Slow." I've noticed that in a great deal of your work—as in J.R.R. Tolkien, C. S. Lewis and some of the best writers of "fantasy" or "science fiction"—there are traces of myths and legends from all over *this* planet, and I noticed particularly the reluctance of certain of your characters to disclose their true names, or "truenames." They show this reluctance much as the California Indian tribes do, I gather.

LE GUIN: Many peoples. Many peoples.

GILBERT: And when they don't reveal their truenames, they don't surrender their identities, or put themselves into someone else's power. And I also noticed traces of cultures from other parts of the world—magicians, kings, the ability of magicians like Festin [in "The Word of Unbinding"] and Ged to transform themselves.

LE GUIN: Yes. Again, that's very widespread, that kind of folk belief.

GILBERT: When you have an idea for a story, do all these ideas for myths in the work come to you at once? How do you sort this out?

LE GUIN: Well, there are several things involved here. One is that science fiction allows a fiction writer to make up cultures, to *invent*—not only a new world, but a new *culture*. Well, what is a culture besides buildings and pots and so on? Of course it's ideas, and ways of thought, and legends. It's all the things that go on inside the heads of the people. So, if you want to make a world and populate it, you also have to make up a civilization and a culture. My father preferred to go find these things; I prefer to invent them. I'm lazier than he was. Of course, where the myths and legends come from is from your own head, the whole thing's coming out of your own head; but it's a sort of combination process of using your intellect to make a coherent-looking body of culture that you can refer to. Tolkien, of course, is the master of this kind of invention. You get the sense in his books of an enormous history, a great body of legend and history and myth all mixed together, which he refers to, so that you get the sense that it really exists. Of course a lot of it *does*, the book he was working on when he died apparently contains a lot of this body of myths. Well, in a sense you have to make it appear as if it were real, but where it comes from is your own unconscious mind, and it's your own myths—the ones you've absorbed and the ones we all—if Jung is right—have within us. We share them. And you're drawing upon your own, your personal mythology.

GILBERT: And the fact that you remember or cherish certain myths from other cultures perhaps means that *those* are your own personal mythology.

LE GUIN: Anybody can hear a story, or read a myth, that hits something deep within them. The ones you remember are the ones that reflect something deep within yourself, which you probably can't put into words, except maybe as a myth. If you're a painter, you could paint it, if you're a musician you could put it into music. But in words you have to do it indirectly. It has to come out as a story.

GILBERT: Have you always done this?

LE GUIN: Well, I got better at it as I went along. [*Laughs*] But yes, I guess so.

GILBERT: Was it hard to learn? It's a complicated art form.

LE GUIN: Well, it just came natural to me. It's obviously the line I always wanted to follow.

GILBERT: Have you ever felt that you had to resist a fascination with a particular culture, or felt that a particular culture was having too great an influence on your work?

LE GUIN: A particular, real, existing earth culture? No, no. Except one is culture-bound. One's own culture is going to dominate one. Again, it seems rather immodest, but science fiction and anthropology do have a good deal in common. As the cultural anthropologist must resist and be conscious of his own cultural limitations, and bigotries, and prejudices—he can't get rid of them, but he must be conscious of them—I think a science fiction writer has a responsibility to do the same thing if he's inventing what he calls a different planet, a different race, alien beings, and so on. His beings can't just be white Anglo-Saxon Protestants with tentacles. You do have to do some rethinking—and [with] a certain self-consciousness of your own bias. But you can't get rid of your limitations; you can't deculturate yourself.

GILBERT: You have, like many poets and writers, a love of names and words, and many of the names you use are extremely evocative. The names are part of the strong spell, for me, of *The Left Hand of Darkness*—names like Karhide, Ehrenrang, Orgoreyn, etc. I suspect you got the last name from Oregon, didn't you?

LE GUIN: No. No, it comes from ogres. Everybody thinks it's rain in Oregon. [*Laughs*] But it's not.

GILBERT: You must be very tired of that assumption.

LE GUIN: Oh, I don't blame people. I just hadn't heard it. [*Pauses to think*] I wanted the vague sense of threat—Orgoreyn sounds slightly threatening to me, and yet it's a rather pretty word. Most of my names mean nothing.

They are not puns, they are not anagrams. They're just pure sound. They just sound right to me.

GILBERT: A pun can be distracting, sometimes.

LE GUIN: Yes. The book becomes a puzzle, instead of a novel.

GILBERT: Do you spend much time sorting out words, testing them? Testing names, that is?

LE GUIN: I have to for the main characters' names. This whole naming magic is partly just a reflection of my own; a reflection of the way I work. If I can't find a character's name, I can't write the book. The name has to be *right*— and when I get the name, it usually means the story's going to come clear. Which is totally mystical; I have no explanation of this whatever.

GILBERT: Do you mean that it's a sort of parallel development? You're thinking of the story, and you're also searching for the name?

LE GUIN: It's as if the name were a key. And I know there's a door there, and if I get the name right, it means I'm going to be able to get the door open, and go on in and find the story on the other side. But why this is so, I have no idea.

GILBERT: And then the other names start going?

LE GUIN: Yes, and the lesser names are always—they're quite easy. And I can change them without doing any harm. But when I wrote *A Wizard of Earthsea*, I had considerable trouble finding what Ged's truename was. And until I found it, I couldn't go on. He had to lose his child's name. Writing that part took—I had a whole page of names.

GILBERT: Do you often make lists of names?

LE GUIN: Oh, yes. Sometimes I think I've found it—*oh, yes, that's it*—but *no, that's not quite right*. [*Laughs*] And then I can't write about this person.

GILBERT: You try a few names for a couple of days?

LE GUIN: Yes. Yes.

GILBERT: Have you a favorite among your books? Maybe that's a terrible question, like asking if you have a favorite among your children, but do you have a favorite work?

LE GUIN: [*Laughs*] Well, in general it's the one that I'm working on, of course, as all writers will admit. I think probably the best put-together book I've written is *A Wizard of Earthsea*. It moves with the most clarity and strength from beginning to end. I think perhaps my favorite of the ones I've written is *The Dispossessed*. I put most into it. It's also the most faulty—probably for that reason—of my grown-up books.

GILBERT: Do you actually think of *The Dispossessed* as an "ambiguous Utopia," as it's described on the cover?

LE GUIN: That was my suggestion. I told the publisher to use that description as a subtitle. They were a little afraid of it, because "ambiguous" is a big word, for one thing. And Utopia does suggest to most of us—*eeeuuuuuw*—you know, dull stories. With morals. And so—one of the publishers used it, one didn't. One of them used it in the blurb for the jacket, or something like that. And I think the English publisher printed it as a subtitle. I just sort of said, if you want to use this as a subtitle, do. Yes, I do think the book is an ambiguous Utopia—in all senses.

GILBERT: I am particularly fond of *The Left Hand of Darkness*; it evokes so many things so well. I like the names, and the evocation of the planet Winter, and the feeling of danger—political danger—of the trip across the ice at the end. Also, of course—I'm sure you've heard this many times—the imagination and daring of creating those androgynous beings. I like that very much.

LE GUIN: It was a very exciting book to write. It was kind of my breakthrough; in my first three science fiction books, I bit off much less, and did much less, and I think that with *The Left Hand of Darkness* I hit my stride, in a way. And it was very exciting to realize how much you could say in science fiction, how much of a real novel you could write. This form does lend itself to the novel, not just to the adventure story. And that was a delight. The Winter part was easy because I'm an Antarctic fan and that grew out of a long obsession with reading Captain Scott's diaries and journals.

GILBERT: Have you been to that kind of country?

LE GUIN: No! As I say, I never left Berkeley until I was seventeen, I'd never seen snow until I went east. That's why I like it so much, I suppose. [*Laughs a little*] But the androgyny part was hard, because I wrote that in 1967, and, as I've said elsewhere, it was when the present feminist movement was just beginning, just getting started. Some of the major books—modern books on feminism—were being written at about that same time, and this apparently was my approach. I'm not a theorist or activist, but—[*pauses to think*]—I wanted to find out what the differences between men and women really were, and so I used this sort of experimental situation of having people who were both men and women at once.

GILBERT: Sorting out new roles.

LE GUIN: Yes, and finding out what it would be like to be a man-woman, or a woman-man. And it was great fun; but it was *rough*, and I had to do a lot of homework on sex roles and on physiology, and on all sorts of things, which was fun. So I did some early feminist reading then, which I'd never done before.

GILBERT: You mean people like Mary Wollstonecraft?

LE GUIN: Yes, and Margaret Mead, and Ashley Montagu, and so on. The books that came just before our modern surge of feminist books. So it was a good education for me.

GILBERT: Did it take you a long time to think up the psychology of the androgynous characters in *The Left Hand of Darkness*?

LE GUIN: It took a long time to work out. For that book I really had to spend about six months, planning the people, the geography, the culture, everything. It was a long time before I could sit down and write the book.

GILBERT: You took notes, then?

LE GUIN: Yes, for that book I really had a notebook full of maps, and history, and all sorts of junk that didn't get into the book—or only got in because I *knew*—you know, you've got to *know*, whether it gets into the book or not, how long the last king reigned and stuff like that.

GILBERT: Yes, I can see that you must work that way. When someone reads your books, or when he reads Tolkien, he feels that there is a whole atmosphere around him, a whole history around him. That's part of the great fascination of the Earthsea books—with their maps of the Archipelago and so on—and of *The Left Hand of Darkness* and *The*

Dispossessed. You're surrounded by all sorts of things that would surround a whole life; you're in a completely different world, but a whole one. Or so it seems.

LE GUIN: Yes. Somehow it's a solid satisfaction, both for writer and reader, I think, to have this totally illusory perception of a non-existent reality. Another odd thing about that book is that—you know those myths that come into it, the little chapters which are local myths and legends?

GILBERT: Some of them very moving.

LE GUIN: They were not meant to go into the book, at first. I would hit snags with these people's psychology, as I was writing the book, and I would think, well, now, how would Therem [Estraven, the main character] really feel about this? And I would be snagged up. So, one of these myths would sort of pop out and write itself, and it would explain something to me, obviously working on a kind of unconscious level. Then I stuck most of them into the book; I finally decided that if they were a help to me they might help the reader, too.

GILBERT: What has been the reaction of readers to those myths, in particular?

LE GUIN: Any novel reader or science fiction reader who is strong on fantasy is particularly fond of that element of the book, because that's where it does run off into myth and fantasy. So those people like it particularly. I think that some of the others wonder what that stuff's in there for.

GILBERT: Yes: I wondered if you got comments like, "I particularly liked the myth of the two young men on the hut on the ice," or "Why do you stop your story and tell us these things?"

LE GUIN: Most of the reaction have been favorable. Most people seem to like those myths, or, if they don't, they're polite and don't tell me.

GILBERT: I am, I must tell you, particularly moved by that myth of the two young princes on the ice. There's the terrifying and beautiful legend of the person who meets the ghost of his brother inside the blizzard; and then there's the legend of the two lovers on the ice.

LE GUIN: That's kind of central to the book. After all, the book is a kind of re-telling of that legend, you see.

GILBERT: Yes. And then the long and dangerous trip over the ice, at the end of the book, is so fascinating. Where you see the old legend evolving again, as if there is an enormous cycle in the culture of the planet Winter and the people in that region of Karhide.

LE GUIN: Yes, that was great fun to write.

GILBERT: Had you thought of the androgynous beings before? How did that idea come to you?

LE GUIN: It came as I was working out this culture which I wanted—one of the original ideas for the book was, I wanted a planet with a lot of cultures on it, a lot of civilizations, a long history, that had never had a major war. This was actually how it began, and the androgyny came secondary to that, to begin with. Then that became a very minor element, once I got the idea that these were androgynes. I wrote a short story about the planet Winter, "Winter's King"; I didn't know yet they were androgynes, when I wrote that.

GILBERT: I've read the most recent version of that story.

LE GUIN: Yes, now I know about the androgynes, and I can put the pronouns into the feminine.

GILBERT: I want to ask you about that. I read that story after I read *The Left Hand of Darkness*, and when I read the novel, I was very much struck by these very convincing people, and I would not have known that a novelist could portray androgynes so convincingly, and I was fascinated. Then I read the story, in which you used the feminine pronoun for the people. It worked for me. I had wondered about using the masculine pronoun, and I guess I thought, as you did, that there was no way around it, other than making up artificial pronouns.

LE GUIN: Which I think you can get by with in a short story; and apparently they don't bother some people; but at the length of a novel, and a serious novel, which is trying to make some point *beside* feminism—and I was—I just think it would drive a normal reader mad. I really do. And I think it would really weaken the book. It weakens the language. You have to work with the language you're given. And thank God it's English. But I'm sorry we don't have a generic pronoun. It makes a great deal of difference. We're trapped with this *he*. Thank goodness for *one*. And you can use *they* a good deal —and I don't mind *they*, I don't care what the English teachers say. I think *they* is often a good road out—instead of *he* or *she*—but you can't always use it.

GILBERT: Can you say something about where you feel your work is going now?

LE GUIN: I have no idea. My most recent book is *A Very Long Way from Anywhere Else*, or *Very Far Away from Anywhere Else*. There was a slight mistake in the title.

GILBERT: Which is the real title?

LE GUIN: The title was meant to be *A Very Long Way From Anywhere Else*, and I simply didn't get it straight with Atheneum. It's not their fault at all, it's my fault. I sent them a preliminary title and didn't realize . . . So in England it's *A Very Long Way* and here it's *Very Far Away*. But it's the same book. It's just a story for young adults, I guess—no fantasy, no science fiction at all. It's just a very short—well, sort of a love story. It's about a high school boy who's bright, which is not a very fashionable subject. But it's very difficult to be bright in high school. And it's about a high school girl who wants to be a composer. And they kind of find each other— you know, how some time along in high school you find another person like yourself. But then there are problems, they have to work out their relationship. And that's all there is to it. It's very short. And it's absolutely straightforward realism, I suppose you'd call it. So, I didn't expect that, I didn't *plan* to write that, no publisher particularly asked for me to write anything like that. It just happened. I like it. I think it came out rather nice. But what happens next, God knows.

GILBERT: Do you like that feeling?

LE GUIN: Yes. Yes. I cannot write to order. I cannot make a deal with a publisher until I can send him a completed manuscript. I can write essays and stuff to order; I learned how to write term papers in college. But writing fiction—I can't. I have to just wait and see what happens.

GILBERT: Have you ever tried to write to order?

LE GUIN: Well, no; I've tried to force myself to write. Just because I wasn't writing, and it was time I wrote something. Well, it was a disaster. It has to *come*. Some of us are just at the mercy of our unconscious, I guess. And of course you control it, and of course you get work habits, and you learn that there is a tap you can turn on; you can sit down at your desk and you can write, *if* you're working on something already. If the initial gift has been given you, then it's your job to write, and that's work, and it takes discipline and so on. But with me, it is a gift, it isn't just something I invent by myself. I wish I could. It'd be nice.

GILBERT: Do you work at home? Do you have a regular schedule?

LE GUIN: Oh, yes. I've met one other professional writer who didn't, and that's Harlan Ellison, because Harlan can write anywhere, anytime, anyplace. You know, in shop windows, at a big New Year's party—Harlan doesn't need a schedule, because he has such enormous energy. And he's free, too. Anyone with the usual commitments and so on— you have to have a schedule. When the kids were little, I worked at night. When they were babies, after they were in bed. When they started going to school, it was while they were at school. So it's sort of nine to one, or nine to twelve.

GILBERT: Do you feel that it has been hard for you to be a writer and, at the same time, fulfill your obligations to your family? Have you found it hard to devote your energies to raising children and to writing?

LE GUIN: Well, yes. There are times, like when I read about Lady Antonia Fraser, with her big books and her five

children and fifteen nursemaids or whatever it is, that I feel
a profound and evil envy. Or when I hear about some man
who has quit a paying job to "devote himself to writing full
time"—I get mean. I think, oh buddy. I wrote when I had
jobs I got paid for; when I quit those, I still had a fulltime
job, the kids and the house, and I still wrote. Who is doing your work for you, Mr. Fulltime Writer? Mrs. Fulltime
Writer? And where are her novels? But all this is mean, as I
said. The fact is, I'm married to a man who has for twenty-
four years ungrudgingly shared the work: the kids, the
house, the whole *schmeer*. Two people *can* do three fulltime
jobs—teaching, writing and family. And when pressed I
will admit that I think this sort of sharing arrangement is
better, though much more tiring, than the fifteen nursemaids, or than hiring help in any way. If I was "free," as so
many male writers have been free, I would be impoverished.
Why should all my time be my own, just because I write
books? There are human responsibilities, and those include
responsibilities to daily life, to common human work. I
mean, cleaning up, cooking, all the work that must be done
over and over all one's life, and also the school concert and
the impossible geometry homework and so on. Responsibility is privilege. If you delegate that work to others, you've
copped out of the very source of your writing, which after
all is life, isn't it, just living, people living and working and
trying to get along.

Well, anyhow, so you get the others off to their work,
at school or college, and you shut the door on the grotty
kitchen and you sit down at your desk and do your work

for a while. Or anyhow you sit there and stare and wish you were doing it. An awful lot of writing seems to be sitting and staring.

GILBERT: Thinking through something.

LE GUIN: Thinking about things; thinking about putting down lousy ideas—

GILBERT: Looking through notebooks?

LE GUIN: Looking through notebooks—exactly. Writing journals if there's nothing better to do. [*Laughs, lights her pipe*]

GILBERT: Do you have strong feelings about where you think science fiction is going?

LE GUIN: I'm a little worried about it, at the moment. A couple of years ago, we were all very hyper. We thought we were really taking off, where we should have been going all along. At the moment, I think we're sort of hesitating. There are some marvelous writers writing now, some of them appreciated, some not—people like Phil Dick, and Stanislaw Lem, D. G. Compton in England; there's absolutely high-class writing being done, as good as any other kind of writing that's being done. It seems to me, though, that there's an increasing amount of schlock being written. That worries me a little. I thought maybe the schlock would taper off. There seems to be an awful lot of young writers who are grinding out the old baloney, and they're going back and using the same old patterns of the 1930s and '40s, which we all thought, a couple of years ago, that we really were outgrowing. There's a great market for this stuff and the demand is going to find the supply somewhere. But I find it a little depressing. An awful lot of publishers really would rather have the schlock, you see.

GILBERT: They think there's a big market for it?

LE GUIN: There is, apparently. It sells, yes. I think there's a bigger market for the good stuff. It may not sell as well at first. It won't sell so well in the drugstores. Look at Phil Dick's books. Phil Dick has never got any publicity, he's never got any real appreciation, very little inside the field, none outside. But his books are all coming back into print, because they are good books, they are first-rate novels. At least five or six or seven of them are absolutely first-rate novels, by any standards, and they are going to stay in print. He's permanent—and science fiction publishers, particularly the paperbacks, aren't used to thinking in terms of permanence. They think in terms of throwaways. And so that's what's got to be changed. And now that science fiction is being used in high schools and colleges, that means the book is going to sell year after year because that's the book the teacher uses. And they've got to keep it in print, and they haven't even realized that yet. They're just beginning to.

GILBERT: And Phil Dick's books, and your books, are being used for these purposes. They're being used in courses all over the place.

LE GUIN: Sure. They're fun to teach. In high school, it's a way to get kids reading. In college they often like to work them into psych courses and sociology courses because they give nice illustrations of points the teacher wants to make. So they're very useful. And I think it's lovely that they're using them that way. It doesn't do anybody any harm, I don't think. [*Laughs*]

"THERE IS MORE THAN ONE WAY TO SEE"

INTERVIEW BY GEORGE WICKES AND LOUISE WESTLING
NORTHWEST REVIEW, VOL. 20, NOS. 2 AND 3
1982

Raj Lyubov is a typical figure in Ursula Le Guin's fiction, an anthropologist whose mission is to report on higher intelligence life forms (HILFs) on another planet. In this case, the planet is populated by a peaceful race of furry human beings three feet tall who live in harmony with the lush forest that covers their world. The men from Earth who have come to log the planet are led by a military macho who regards these "creechies" as subhuman and treats them brutally. Le Guin has explained that she wrote *The Little Green Men* (as she entitled it) in protest against the Vietnam War in which the landscape was defoliated and noncombatants of a different race were callously slaughtered in the name of peace and humanity. Characteristically in this novel she subordinates science fiction to her liberal humanitarianism and her concern for the natural world of which humanity is but a part.

Anthropology came naturally to the daughter of the great Berkeley anthropologist Alfred Kroeber and his wife Theodora, a writer best known for her biography of Ishi, the last surviving Indian of his tribe. Writing also came easily to Ursula Le Guin, but success did not come until she turned her talents to science fiction and fantasy. Then she published in rapid succession three novels set in the universe she was to explore in later novels, and the first volume in the Earthsea trilogy which introduced still another world, this time an antique world of wizards and dragons and legends. Since 1966 Le Guin has published more than a dozen novels and won some of the most prestigious literary awards. Her most highly acclaimed novels are *The Left Hand of Darkness* and *The Dispossessed*.

The interview was conducted in the Le Guin family home in Portland, a comfortable old wooden house on the edge of Forest Park. The neighborhood seems an appropriate setting for the author who created the forest world of Athshe. In collecting her stories for publication in *The Wind's Twelve Quarters* she discovered "a certain obsession with trees" in her writing and concluded that she is "the most arboreal science fiction writer." She talks a bit about this dendrophilia in the interview.

GEORGE WICKES: When did you first know that you were going to be a writer?

URSULA K. LE GUIN: I don't know. I sort of took it as an established fact.

WICKES: From infancy?

LE GUIN: Yes. When I learned how to write, apparently.

WICKES: What do you suppose it is that makes people write fiction?

LE GUIN: They want to tell a story.

WICKES: There's much more than story in your fiction.

LE GUIN: But I think the basic impulse is probably to tell a story. And why we do that I don't quite know.

LOUISE WESTLING: Did you write lots of stories as a child?

LE GUIN: Some. I wrote a lot of poetry. They've always gone together. But I started writing stories somewhere around eight or nine, I think, when I got an old typewriter. Somehow the typewriter led me to prose—although I don't compose on the typewriter now.

WESTLING: What kind of books were your favorites in early life?

LE GUIN: I grew up in a professor's house lined with books. My favorites as a child were certainly fiction or narrative, novels and myths and legends and all that. But I read a lot of popular science, too, as a kid. Altogether, pretty much what I read now.

WICKES: If you were asked to compile a list of the books that have been most important to you, not only as a writer but also in your thinking, what would be the first half dozen?

LE GUIN: I tried to do it, and it goes on and on. It's

insufferably boring, because I've read all my life, and I read everything. I've been so influenced by so much that as soon as I mention one name I think, "Oh, but I can't say that without saying that." I think there are certain obvious big guns, but I really hate to say any one, or six, or twenty. But you could very roughly say that the English novelists of the nineteenth century and the Russian novelists of the twentieth century were formative. That's where my love and admiration and emulation was when I started. But then I read all that other junk, too. And I did my college work in French and Italian literature. I never much liked the French novelists. I can tell you what I *don't* like. I don't much like "the great tradition," the James-Conrad thing that I was supposed to like when I was in college. I've revolted against that fairly consciously. Flaubert I really consider a very bad model for a fiction writer.

WICKES: Stendahl?

LE GUIN: Stendahl's a good novelist, but I think the limitations of Stendahl have been rather disastrous. I think you'd do better with Balzac. If you have to imitate a Frenchman.

WESTLING: Proust?

LE GUIN: You can't imitate Proust. And in modern writing, for instance, Nabokov means nothing to me. I have great trouble reading him. I see a certain lineage there which I just don't follow, don't have any sympathy for.

WICKES: How about more philosophical books, like some of the Oriental thinkers, or Thoreau?

LE GUIN: You'll find him buried around in poems and novels fairly frequently, but I don't know Thoreau very well. You have to be a New Englander to really read Thoreau. There was stuff around the house, again. My father's favorite book was a copy of Lao Tzu, and seeing it in his hands a lot, I as a kid got interested. Of course, it's very accessible to a kid, it's short, it's kind of like poetry, it seems rather simple. And so I got into that pretty young, and obviously found something that I wanted, and it got very deep into me. I have fits of delving further into Oriental thought. But I have no head for philosophy.

WESTLING: You've said that you now associate some of your ideas with Jung but that you probably came to these yourself first before you ever read Jung.

LE GUIN: My father was a Freudian—he was a lay analyst—so the word *Jung* was a four-letter word in our household. After the Earthsea trilogy was published, people kept telling me, "Oh, this is wonderful, you've used Jung's shadow." And I'd say, "It's not Jung's shadow, it's my shadow." But I realized I had to read him, and then I got fascinated. Then he was extremely helpful to me as a shaman or guide at a rather difficult point in my life. At the moment I wouldn't want to read Jung; you have to need him, like most psychologists. But it was amazing to me to find how parallel in certain places his imagination and my imagination, or his observation and my imagination, had run.

WESTLING: Well, part of it could be your absorption with mythology, because he came to his thinking by saturating himself in mythology.

LE GUIN: I didn't have an absorption with mythology, but I had a child's curiosity, and there were Indian legends all over the place. My father told us stories that he had learned from his informants, and my mother was interested, too. The books I read were mostly children's editions, but what's the difference? The stories are there.

WESTLING: Yes, it doesn't matter, the pattern is what counts.

WICKES: How do your books come to you? Is there a particular process, or is it different every time?

LE GUIN: It varies from book to book. For some of them it's very neat, and I can describe the process, but then for another one it's utterly different. *Left Hand of Darkness* is the nicest one because it came as a vision, a scene of these two people pulling something in a great snowy wilderness. I simply knew that there was a novel in it. As Angus Wilson describes it, his books come that way, with a couple of people in a landscape. But some of them don't come that easy at all. *The Dispossessed* came with a perfectly awful short story, one of the worst things I ever wrote. There it was, all about prison camps, everything in it all backwards, a monstrosity of a little story. Then I thought, "You know, it's really terrible that you could write anything that bad after writing all these years; there's got to be something in it." And sure enough, there was, after about two years' work and reading all these utopists and all the anarchists and thinking a lot. That one took real homework. But sure enough, the idea had been there all along; I just hadn't understood it. Yes, I worked like all the blazes on that one. And for *Left Hand of Darkness* I had to plan that world with extreme care, writing its history, roughly, before I could do a good solid novel.

WICKES: It seems to me there's a good deal of geography in your writing, too.

LE GUIN: I like geography and geology. You may notice the other thing besides trees is rocks.

WICKES: Yes, and landscapes, weathers, climates—you go into these things a great deal.

LE GUIN: It's one reason I adore Tolkien; he always tells you what the weather is, always. And you know pretty well where north is, and what kind of landscape you're in and so on. I really enjoy that. That's why I like Hardy. Again, you always know what the weather is.

WESTLING: You said you liked trees and you liked rocks, and that expresses a dichotomy I've felt in your fiction, between lush forest worlds and desolate places where people have to struggle. I wonder whether you are simply a creechie but are restrained by pioneer impulses.

LE GUIN: You know, I've had this mad fascination with Antarctica ever since I was sixteen or seventeen and first read [polar explorer Robert Falcon] Scott, and that's where all that snow and ice comes in. I believe all the sledge trips in *Left Hand of Darkness* are accurate. That was very important to me; that I didn't give them too much to pull and make them go too far.

WESTLING: That's the heart of that book, the most fully realized thing in it.

LE GUIN: Sure, that's where it started. But that is also my Antarctic dream, my having followed Scott and [Edward] Wilson on those awful trips for years. Every now and then I have another binge, going back to Antarctica. I have a story coming out in the *New Yorker* about the first women who got to Antarctica. Actually, they got to the Pole first. But they didn't leave any traces.

WICKES: You mean they got there ahead of everyone else?

LE GUIN: They got there just a little ahead of Amundsen. A small group of South American women. I think I enjoyed writing that story ["Sur"] more than anything in my whole life.

WICKES: Now that brings up something else. You have all these journeys in your fiction; people are always traveling around. That's a great way to see your geography, but it often becomes the plot. We go on a journey, not always an ordeal or quest, but we always go on a journey.

LE GUIN: You've just hit a very significant note here. Actually I'm terrible at plotting, so all I do is sort of put people in motion and they go around in a circle and they generally end up about where they started out. That's a Le Guin plot.

WESTLING: Well, who says you have to go straight ahead and then stop?

LE GUIN: I admire real plotting, the many strands and real suspense. But I seem not able to achieve it.

WESTLING: Have feminists commended you on this fact? They should. That's supposed to be feminine, just as Eastern culture is supposed to be feminine because it emphasizes the circular.

LE GUIN: But complexity surely is neither masculine nor feminine, and I see the line of my stories being awfully simple. It's not that I want to write mysteries, I'm talking about something more like what Dickens did, pulling strands together, weaving something—I'm not very good at that. I just plunge ahead. Or I do it by trickery, by zigzagging.

WICKES: How long have you lived in Oregon?

LE GUIN: Since 1959.

WICKES: Do you think Oregon has had an influence on your work?

LE GUIN: Sure. It's the place I've lived longest now.

WICKES: Has it made you a dendrophile, or were you one already?

LE GUIN: I must have been one already, but I didn't even notice until I was looking over that bunch of short stories I was supposed to write an introduction for and suddenly realized, "My God, this thing's crawling with trees." I think living on the edge of a forest has had some influence. And we've managed to plant a forest, without really intending to. The kids won't let us cut anything down: "Oh, what a sweet little seedling!" So now we have a garden towering over us. And every summer when I was growing up in northern California, I lived in a forest, up in the foothills of Napa Valley, and going out in the woods was what I did.

WESTLING: Were you a tomboy?

LE GUIN: I had three older brothers, so I tagged around after them. I wasn't brave, and I didn't climb trees—I've been terrified of climbing and so on—I was not a tomboy in the sense of being brave and courageous, but my parents made no great distinctions between boys and girls, so I had the freedom of the woods.

WICKES: Would your feelings about nature have something to do with your feelings about what we might loosely call civilization or more exactly call technology? How do you feel about technology—for or against?

LE GUIN: Oh, for. I don't know, it's such a large question, every answer turns out sounding like a fortune cookie, but you don't get civilizations of any kind without technology. If you want a tool to do something with, you've got to figure out how to make it and how to make it best. And all that aspect of life I enjoy very much. I am really interested in things and artifacts, doings and makings and objects. So in the very simplest sense I enjoy technology. I love a good tool or a well-made thing.

WICKES: Yes, but there's a difference between craftsmanship and technology.

LE GUIN: Well, craftsmanship is just good technology. Now if you're talking about the excesses of the industrial West, then obviously we have taken something too far too hard. But to say that I'm against technology would make me a Luddite, and that I detest and abhor and am afraid of. People who think they can get on without the things that we now know how to do are kidding themselves. I would last five days in the woods without a good deal of technology. And besides, I like houses and cities.

WICKES: Yet it seems to me that your ideal state is the one you describe in *City of Illusions*, for instance, a comfortable old Maybeck house in the forest, with modern conveniences that nobody has to look after, where life is rather simple.

LE GUIN: No, no, not at all. That's a total dead end. That's why he had to get out of that place. It was fun to describe it, to give it the solar cells and stuff so they had this nice, low-level dream technology, but I'm a city person.

WICKES: I'm surprised to hear you say that because I thought the city was a bad place in your fiction. There's the one in *City of Illusions*, which is a bad place, or the one on Urras in *The Dispossessed*, which is beautiful and luxurious but ultimately evil.

LE GUIN: But what about the other city in that book, the one on Annares? It's a kind of Paul Goodman city.

WESTLING: And yet dangers lurk there, because of the political conniving.

LE GUIN: A city is where all dangers come together for human beings, where everything happens to human beings. I use "city" in a fairly metaphorical sense. A city is where culture comes together and flowers. A pueblo is a city.

WESTLING: The idyllic moments in many of your stories, though, seem to occur outside of cities. It's the pastoral problem. People need to escape the corruption of urban life and find renewal in an idealized natural setting, but they have to go back.

LE GUIN: Yes, people are always going back and forth. But in my fiction the place they're going to end up and do their work and live their lives out is the city. As at the end of *The Beginning Place*, which is, of course, much fresher in my mind than *City of Illusions* is. If I might say so, *City of Illusions* is rather a bad book to use for anything; it's my least favorite and certainly the one with the most just plain stupid mistakes and holes in it.

WICKES: Still, quite often you present this antithesis between the modern city and the natural world, and my impression is that your fiction doesn't show much interest in technology. By technology I mean hardware, gadgetry. This side of science fiction doesn't seem to interest you very much, and though you've got the convenience of space travel which will permit you to visit all these wonderful different worlds, you're not really interested in how the contraption works.

LE GUIN: Not at all. Because I don't believe in it. If you ask me, do I believe that we will have space-flight of the speed necessary to get outside the solar system in any *foreseeable* future, I'd say no. We have nothing leading to such technology. So the whole thing is a metaphor, and you play around with making it look realistic, because that's part of the fun of a novel. And I put limitations like they couldn't exceed the speed of light. I like that part of it; I like playing with theory and what science I am able to absorb, which is pretty limited. But the engineering part is where I draw the line. I like my washing machine, and I treat it well, but I don't really yearn to know what's inside.

WESTLING: How do you go about mapping out an imaginary world like that of *Malafrena*?

LE GUIN: You certainly have to have maps. You have to know how far it is from there to there, or you get all mushy in your mind. Don't all the novelists draw maps? Jane Austen did it, when she needed to, and the Brontës did.

WESTLING: But when Joyce wrote back to Dublin and had people measure the time it would take to walk from one place to another and whether Bloom could jump over the railings, wasn't he being awfully literal-minded?

LE GUIN: Well, of course. A novelist has to be really, stupidly literal about these things.

WICKES: But that's very different from inventing a country, as you do in *Malafrena*.

LE GUIN: Whether it's real Dublin or invented Dublin, it's got to be right. Whether it's really there and other people can walk it, or whether you're building it for them to walk in the mind, it's got to be absolutely solid.

WESTLING: When you got ready to write *The Lathe of Heaven*, did you wander around in downtown Portland to see exactly where the parking structure was in relation to the other places?

LE GUIN: I checked a couple of things, because my memory's so terrible. There are deliberate red herrings there. For instance, I could show you the house George lives in, but it's not on the street I say it is, it's one down. And Dave's Delicatessen never was on Ankeny Street. When they moved it, I went into an absolute panic. I thought, if they put it on Ankeny, I'm leaving this town.

WICKES: Why did you choose Portland as the setting instead of some imaginary place?

LE GUIN: Oh, that wasn't an imaginary place type of story. That was about America now. That story came close to home, literally.

WICKES: Is this your vision of what's going to happen in the next twenty years?

LE GUIN: The book's a dream, quite a bad one. If I had a vision of what's going to happen, I'm sure I would be unable to speak of it. And I don't see why I should. I don't see what right I have. I'm not a prophet. I do not predict. I certainly hope I'm wrong.

WICKES: Are you more interested in the past or in the future? Your fiction goes both ways.

LE GUIN: It's all mixed up together for me. You don't get one without the other. It's a Gordian knot which I have no wish to cut. It's obvious there's going to be no future without the past and no past without the future. I get rather Chinese about the whole thing.

WESTLING: Well, in a way then, real time doesn't matter because what you're doing is establishing metaphors within which problems can be explored. Is that right?

LE GUIN: Yes. And I think the way of talking about time that makes the most sense to me and within which I work most happily is to connect what it's now fashionable to call waking-time and dream-time. There are two aspects of time, and we live waking in one; but Western Civilization has announced that there's only one real time, and it is that one. This I more or less consciously reject, and I am perpetually attempting by one metaphor and device or another in my books to reestablish the connection between the dream-time and the waking-time, to say that the one depends upon the other absolutely.

WESTLING: Well, then, do you see the writer as a dreamer?

LE GUIN: Any artist goes back and forth between the two times, trying to speak one to the other, as a translator or interpreter.

WICKES: One of the most interesting things that keeps turning up again and again in your fiction is "mindspeech" and telepathy. Do you believe in ESP or anything like that?

LE GUIN: I have to give an agnostic's answer. I certainly have never experienced it. But it was a very convenient metaphor for what I needed to do in the stories. I am not sure what it's a metaphor for. I've read some critics who have had some ideas about what I was trying to say and have left that to them because I really don't know what I was babbling about. I just know I needed it in certain stories.

WICKES: I think it works very well.

LE GUIN: It certainly is another way of talking about double vision. There is more than one way to see, more than one way to speak, more than one aspect to reality.

WESTLING: It's also a way to indicate the closeness of the two travelers across the ice.

LE GUIN: Sure, it's a lovely emotional metaphor. You can play with it endlessly. That's what's so neat about science fiction. It gives you the opportunity to say, "All right, there is such a thing as telepathy, and you can learn it as a technique." Then you play with it novelistically. That's why I've enjoyed writing science fiction.

WESTLING: Have you ever lived in a desolate place like Anarres?

LE GUIN: No, I never really lived in a desert, although I'd been across it in a train, until we went to [the eastern Oregon town of] Frenchglen years ago, just overnight. A whole book, *The Tombs of Atuan*, came out of that one trip into the Oregon desert. And I'm absolutely addicted to the desert now. Both of my parents liked the high desert country; they liked the Southwest and went there when they could.

WESTLING: Your new story in the *New Yorker* makes me think of another question, which I'm sure you've been asked ad nauseum, but I'll just ask it one more time. Why is it that most of your protagonists are male?

LE GUIN: I don't know. Yes, I've certainly been asked it, and I've tried and tried to answer it, and I've given up trying to answer it. In the crudest sense it's that all protagonists doing the kinds of things that I had mine doing were male, and it took an effort of the imagination which I wasn't capable of making until very recently to change that. This is going to look rather odd in print, but it really doesn't matter to me very much what sex people are, and this is my main problem as a feminist. Every now and then I forget to be upset.

WESTLING: Well, Flannery O'Connor said that she always knew there were two sexes, but she guessed that she behaved as if there were only one.

LE GUIN: Yes, I'm afraid this happens to a lot more of us than has either been fashionable or even right to admit, but I think now we can admit it. I think the Movement has gone far enough, given us strength enough that we can say it. Sometimes it just doesn't bloody matter.

WESTLING: I used to be quite disturbed when I thought of myself in front of a classroom. For years I saw a man in a tweed coat with a pipe. And that bothered me. I've been working on it for ten years, and I'm still not able to see me up there yet, but it's not the man in the tweed coat anymore. I wonder whether you've had to make that kind of conscious effort.

LE GUIN: Oh, yes. And I am so grateful to the whole women's movement for giving me the intellectual tools to make the effort with. Sometimes it's almost gimmicks—making yourself change the sex of a pronoun to see what happens, for example.

WESTLING: So sex does matter, ultimately, doesn't it?

LE GUIN: Of course it does. But it doesn't always matter in everything.

WESTLING: Well, if one grows up with adventure stories, they're always about boys, and one's imagination gets formed by that.

LE GUIN: That's it. But you see, I happily identified totally with the hero—if it was *Jane Eyre*, I identified with her; if it was a hero in Zane Grey, I identified with him—and I never thought a thing about it. And so I didn't think anything about it as a writer. My conscience had to be raised a lot before I saw that. As of about the early seventies, it does matter. Now I can't do this innocently anymore, that innocence is gone. So now it matters a lot what one's protagonist is. I would defend my earlier books, because then it didn't matter. But now it does.

WESTLING: So you wouldn't agree with Virginia Woolf that there is such a thing as a woman's prose style.

LE GUIN: I don't know. I am not going to disagree with Virginia Woolf about anything. I see her style, which is wonderful. Now there's the kind of complexity that I envy with my whole heart, that kind of weaving. But is there anybody besides Virginia Woolf who can do that particular sort of thing? You see, that way of thinking slides so easily into a sort of sexism that it worries me a bit.

WESTLING: But many of your stories are about hero adventures in the vein of the old military epics with hardly any participation by women.

LE GUIN: Are they? Well, particularly the earlier ones. There's nothing like a good vicarious adventure.

WICKES: Speaking of one of the later ones, when did you write *Malafrena*? At the time it was published [in 1979], or was this a book you'd written earlier?

LE GUIN: No, it wasn't a book I'd written earlier, but parts of it are very old. The idea and some bits of it go back to the mid-fifties or late fifties. And it shows in the way it's put together; it creaks a little. It's a very old-fashioned novel. It's a nineteenth-century novel.

WICKES: We would have guessed that it was your apprentice work.

LE GUIN: Well, there's apprentice work in it.

WICKES: Of course it's entirely appropriate that it should be a nineteenth-century novel; it's right in the tradition of Stendhal.

LE GUIN: If you're going to write about the revolution of 1830, you might as well do so in a style appropriate to the subject.

WICKES: You majored in Romance languages in college. What other languages do you know at least something of? The reason I ask is that you have these names that seem to be part Germanic, part Slavic, part Scandinavian.

LE GUIN: Well, I've got a little linguistic facility which I haven't done much with. I'm trying to teach myself Spanish now, but that's no great trouble for someone with French and Italian. I didn't learn any other languages. But my father was an ethnologist. There were books about language around, and he talked with informants in the languages he knew, like Yurok. The house was always full of people with funny accents. I'm comfortable with foreign languages, and I enjoy them, so it's a lot of fun making them up. Word-making is one of the roots of fantasy. It reaches its peak in Tolkien, who said he wrote *The Lord of the Rings* so that they could say "Good morning" in Elvish.

WICKES: How do you choose your names? It seems to me you have a hodgepodge, or is that deliberate?

LE GUIN: I don't think you'll find too much hodgepodge in the phonemes of any language that is implied by the names in a certain island or a certain country in my books. I tried to have fairly clear in mind what pool of sounds they used because it bothers me very much in other people's fantasies when they have a hodgepodge of sounds that don't go together. One name obviously resembles German and the next something totally different, like Chinese, and then you get an "X," which you don't know how to pronounce. I tried for a certain coherence in implied language, and also for something that looks pronounceable to the reader so that he doesn't have to stop every time he comes to it.

WICKES: In Earthsea you've got quite a variety in the names.

LE GUIN: Well, there are four languages going in Earthsea. There's Kargad; there's Hardic, the main one; there's the Old Language, and then there's the language they speak up in Osskil.

WICKES: Then in *Malafrena* you have characters with names taken from several different languages. I spent a lot of time trying to figure out where Orsinia was, and whether you agree or not, I know it's Hungary.

LE GUIN: Well, it isn't Hungary, but it must be pretty near Hungary. I'll tell you something funny. I've been told quite authoritatively by several people what it is and where it is, and nobody has ever mentioned Czechoslovakia, which is incredible to me because it seems fairly obvious that there's a lot of resemblance. Could I throw Romania at you? That's the language.

WICKES: Well, I figured it should be Romania, but it doesn't fit. For me the real clincher is that when Luisa goes to Vienna she stays in the Hotel König von Ungarn.

LE GUIN: You know why? Because I stayed in the König von Ungarn. It was right behind the [cathedral]. It's closed now, but it was a real hotel that Mozart and Beethoven stayed in, so I could use it with total assurance. I knew it was there in the 1820s and 1830s.

WICKES: Do you attach any particular significance to the names in *Malafrena*? For instance, Valtorskar and Paludeskar seem to be landscape names. Is there a significance to those landscapes? Is Luisa a swamp?

LE GUIN: There's a touch of swampiness in the Paludeskar family. I like Luisa, though. Now that was one of the parts of the book that was old. Luisa was an incredible villainess as I first thought about her, the *femme fatale*, when I was trying to write that book way back when.

WICKES: One final question. What are you writing now?

LE GUIN: I have just been working on a television screenplay of one of my short stories for PBS. This is a new venture for me, screenwriting. Last year I was working on a screenplay for Earthsea with Michael Powell. He's an old British director—have you seen *The Red Shoes*?—and he was determined to make Earthsea into a movie.

WESTLING: And what's its fate?

LE GUIN: Its fate is Hollywood. We wrote a perfectly

beautiful screenplay that would make a beautiful, serious fantasy, finally, in the movies. But then Hollywood said, "Oh, yes, this is wonderful, yes, we want to do this, but actually what we need now is a movie about immortality." And so Michael and I said, "Well, yes, but you see, what we have is not a movie about immortality. We have a movie about this here wizard, and this young lady." We did the whole thing backwards. You never start with a script. What we should have done is gone down to Hollywood together, Michael and me, and said, "Here we are, you're going to buy us, for $200,000, and two years from now we will give you the script that you always wanted." What idiots, we arrived with a script! And so now they want to rewrite it. And it's going to be our movie or no movie. So it will probably be no movie. But we are both rather obstinate people, and we believe in our screenplay; so who knows?

IN A WORLD OF HER OWN

INTERVIEW BY NORA GALLAGHER
MOTHER JONES
JANUARY 1984

Ursula Kroeber Le Guin lives in Portland, Oregon, in an old house that looks down on the shipyards and docks of the Williamette River. The house is clean and very spare: in the upstairs bedrooms (the Le Guins have three children, all of whom have left home), each bed is covered with a simple cotton cover, each floor has a single rug. At the end of the upstairs hallway, behind a door usually kept closed, is a tiny room, once a nursery, with French windows opening out to the tops of trees—hawthorn, pear, apple, willow. Within this room, for the past twenty years, Le Guin has been inventing and constructing whole worlds of her own.

On the wall above a narrow day bed, pieces of graph paper hang from large metal clips. On one, in Le Guin's neat, penciled hand, is a map: two fingers of land interrupted by a sea. This is northern California, the author explains, and part of Nevada with the Central Valley in between, under water. Covering this sketch, on a sheet of transparent paper, are the familiar towns of the Napa Valley—St. Helena, Calistoga, Yountville—as well as the Sierra and lava beds in the northeast of the state. This map is only for reference so that Le Guin will not make a gross error when she describes the distances between the very unfamiliar towns—Sinshan and Wakwaha and Chumo—on a third sheet overlaying the other two. The maps are the working papers for Le Guin's book-in-progress, which takes place sometime in the near future, after earthquakes and continental shift have destroyed San Francisco, sunk Bakersfield, and given the Humboldt River in Nevada an outlet to the sea.

In this book, Le Guin has come home, using as her central location the Napa Valley, where she has spent the summer for fifty of her fifty-four years. It has been a long homecoming. Of all her novels, this will be one of the few that takes place on Earth.

Ursula Kroeber Le Guin has been writing stories ever since an older brother taught her to write. In the past twenty years, she has published fourteen novels, three books of short stories, a book of essays and two books of poems; she has collaborated on two screenplays and has written a television script of her novel *The Lathe of Heaven*. She has won four Hugo awards, three Nebula awards, a Newbery Honor Book Citation and a National Book Award. She is considered by many critics and readers to be the best writer of fantasy and science fiction in America today. But science fiction, at least as we have known it and although she has often passionately defended the genre, is not quite what Le Guin does. "I write science fiction because that is what publishers call my books," she once wrote. "Left to myself, I should call them novels."

The appeal of science fiction lies in its subject: the "Other"—the alien world, the stuff of dreams, the raw material from the unconscious. Because these things are contained in a story with a beginning, a middle and end, they are less terrifying than they might be if we met them on the street or in our nightmares. But what most American science fiction did before the late 1950s, when Le Guin's generation of science fiction writers began to publish, was to present the Other and then immediately defeat it: the aliens always got theirs in the end; the lean, square-jawed space captain shot his way through the swarm of bug-eyed monsters (with the dumb blonde clinging to his muscular arm); and the whole galaxy was made safe for free enterprise. Probably more than any other writing, science fiction reflected the mood of America: if it's different, kill it.

To this world, Le Guin has brought, well, first she has brought women: a black lawyer in *The Lathe of Heaven*; a marine biologist in *The Dispossessed*; a grocery clerk in *The Beginning Place*. Her aliens tend to be bewildered, obsessive, or just plain tired. In *The Lathe of Heaven*, her alien lives over a bicycle repair shop in Portland and runs a tacky secondhand store that sells, among other things, old Beatles records. Le Guin has introduced themes risky in any American novel: anarchism as social and economic alternative, socialism, feminism, Taoism, environmentalism, love and suffering. In one wonderful story, she swept up the male image of a spaceship and sex-changed it: "Intracom" is about a small space vessel that finds it has an alien onboard. The alien? A fetus. The ship, a pregnant woman.

In her novels, the human scale is always kept intact; all other things are measured against it. No fantastic technology takes the place of a human hand or heart: "Community is the best we can hope for," Le Guin wrote in her essay

"Science Fiction and Mrs. Brown," "and community for most people means *touch*: the touch of your hand against the other's hand, the job done together, the sledge hauled together, the dance danced together, the child conceived together. We have only one body apiece, and two hands."

Last summer, I spent three days in Portland talking to Le Guin: on the small deck of the house overlooking the river, over dinner at Jake's (a wood-paneled restaurant famous for its crawfish), in the middle of a demonstration on Hiroshima Day, and standing ankle-deep in the Columbia River watching the wash from a ship. We were joined often by her husband, Charles, a professor of French history at Portland State University, a generous Southern man to whom she has dedicated two of her books. "For Charles," she wrote in *The Left Hand of Darkness*, "*sine quo non*"— without whom, nothing.

Le Guin is a smallish person with large intelligent eyes, her gray hair cut into a neat cap. On the first day we talked, she was wearing a purple silk blouse, a raw silk skirt and delicate shoes. She has a low, direct voice and while there is about her an air of grave authority, she is also likely to burst into the accents of a French professor, a Cockney maid, a Scottish cook. At a speech she gave in London, she wore a formal black velvet suit and a propeller beanie. She has described herself as "a petty-bourgeois anarchist," "an unconsistent Taoist and consistent unChristian." What is morality, I asked her once, and she replied: "Something you grope after when a situation comes up in which it's needed."

• • •

The Left Hand of Darkness, which won both the Hugo and Nebula science-fiction awards, is set in another galaxy, but it is about two very human problems: betrayal and fidelity. (When asked once what the most constant theme in her novels was, she replied, without stopping to think twice, "Marriage.")

The book grew out of Le Guin's increasing involvement in feminism. "Along about 1967, I began to feel a certain unease, a need to step on a little farther, perhaps, on my own," she wrote in her essay "Is Gender Necessary?" "I began to want to define and understand the meaning of sexuality and the meaning of gender, in my life and in our society. Much had been gathered in the unconscious—both personal and collective—which must either be brought up into consciousness, or else turn destructive. It was the same need, I think, that had led Beauvoir to write *The Second Sex*, and Friedan to write *The Feminine Mystique*; and that was, at the same time, leading Kate Millett and others to write their books, and to create the new feminism. But I was not a theoretician, a political thinker or activist, or a sociologist. I was and am a fiction writer. The way I did my thinking was to write a novel. That novel, *The Left Hand of Darkness*, is the record of my consciousness, the process of my thinking."

At the center of her thinking the question became: What would a planet be like if it didn't have any wars? How would the people differ from us? What would they have or lack? Over time, she began to realize that the people of her book would be neither male nor female, but both. Thus the "Gethenians" were born: sexual androgynes, bisexuals, sexual possibles. Once a month, like other animals, they enter into a kind of heat, when their bodies change and polarize, become male or female. No one knows which he/she will be. If conception occurs, the female remains female and bears a child. If not, she returns to androgyny. The mother of one child could be the father of several others. (Le Guin says she never really knew whether this was actually physiologically possible in humans until she gave the completed manuscript to her pediatrician, a Frenchman, to read. "It is perfectly possible," he told her, "but it is disgusting.")

There is no rape on Gethen, no division of labor between "weak women" and "strong men," and since at any time one may bear and raise a child, no males quite so free as males elsewhere. There are also no wars. There are skirmishes, raids, quarrels over territory, but no huge troop movements over continents. A pregnant person does not a general make.

The hero of the book, a visitor from Earth, is very uncomfortable with this arrangement, and it is his gradual, painful discovery of love between equals that forms the book's heart. Le Guin has been criticized for using a male hero, but she has an explanation: "I knew a woman would just love it. There wouldn't be any dramatic scenes; she would just settle right down. I needed this guy who hated it, who was uncomfortable and miserable in it. It's true, a woman wouldn't have done. She would have just run around saying, 'Oooh, this is wonderful.'"

Le Guin did not know all this when she began the novel. For her, it started with a vision of two people pulling something across a lot of snow, and much of its content was "told to her" by the characters as she went along. Once she discovered something about them, she would go back over the novel, changing pieces here and there.

"The first time I ever went to a meeting where they discussed any of my books academically," she chuckled, "a Canadian scholar was going to discuss *The Left Hand of Darkness*. He didn't know that I was going to be there. When I walked in, he was appalled. He looked at me with a savage look on his face and said, 'Just don't tell me you didn't know what you were doing.' That's a basic thing, actually, between scholars and artists. I think, *'Oh, is that what I was doing? Or Is that why I did that?* and it's very revealing. But the fact is, you cannot know that while you're doing it. The dancer can't think, *Now I'm going to take a step to the left.* That ain't the way you dance."

• • •

We ate a dinner of cold salmon from the Columbia Gorge, sitting at a picnic table on the broad porch that encircles the rear of the house, "leftovers" from a farewell dinner Le Guin had made for her daughter Caroline the night before. (Caroline was returning to Indiana, where she is starting her doctorate in Irish literature.) On the table was a small cup holding little silver spoons, very soft, very high-quality silver, commemorative pieces minted in different towns in

Colorado during the great silver mining days. They were collected by Le Guin's mother, Theodora; one was from Telluride, where she grew up.

Theodora met and married Alfred Kroeber in Berkeley, where he was a professor of anthropology at the university and she was his student (he remembered her bracelets clinking together when she spoke in class). Alfred is perhaps most well-known for his work and friendship with Ishi, a Stone Age man, the last of his tribe, who stumbled into the twentieth century in 1911. (Ishi died of tuberculosis in 1916, when he was probably fifty-six.) But it was Theodora Kroeber who, in her sixties, wrote the book *Ishi In Two Worlds*, which became nearly as popular as *Coming of Age in Samoa* and is considered a standard text in anthropology.

Much of Le Guin's feeling for the Other, the anthropological details in her books and her fierce devotion to a balanced way of living on the earth, can be traced to her early upbringing. Although the name Ishi was never mentioned in the house (the subject seemed to cause Alfred Kroeber pain), Ursula heard Native American stories and myths from her father. And she remembers him sitting and talking to two of his closest friends, one a Papago and the other a Yurok, men who, unbeknownst to her then, were also her father's anthropological informants, and who stayed with the family in the Napa Valley each summer and played croquet with Ursula and her three older brothers.

There were other guests: refugees with funny accents, other Native Americans, and a man with large ears who would "reappear" in her novel *The Dispossessed*: J. Robert Oppenheimer.*

Ishi was published in 1961, a year after Alfred Kroeber's death. The book is so well written that Ursula, stricken with guilt, asked her mother if she had been unable to write earlier because of having to raise children. Her mother replied, "I did what I wanted when I wanted to. I have long thought I'd write when I wanted to." She was, said Le Guin, "a very unusual person."

Le Guin went to Berkeley High School, which she hated. "I wasn't—you know, I never—my sweaters were never quite the right length or color. I never could do it right." She then went to Radcliffe, and later Columbia, where she earned an M.A. in French, figuring she would need a skill to support herself while writing. She had already submitted poems and short stories by the time she went off to college—her father volunteered to be her agent. Some of the poems got published, but all of the short stories came back. These rejections went on until she was twenty-seven, short, civil notes; the characteristic adjective used by editors at *Redbook* and *Harper's* and *The Atlantic* was "remote." But Le Guin was not particularly discouraged: "I was dogged," she says now. "I had an absolutely unfounded self-confidence, partly a temperamental thing and the way my parents brought me up. And I knew that I would get better."

She met Charles Le Guin in 1953 on the *Queen Mary*

---

* A professor of theoretical physics at Cal, Oppenheimer ran the Los Alamos nuclear lab during World War II and is considered the father of the atomic bomb.

when both were sailing to France on Fulbright scholarships. After the crossing, Le Guin was "fairly sure." The two married in France and returned at the end of the year to Macon, Georgia, where Charles had grown up.

There, in the bosom of a huge Southern family ("There are hundreds and hundreds of them," says Le Guin), Charles finished his doctorate and Ursula taught freshman French. She continued writing: she wrote a novel while she was working, once, as a secretary in the physics department of Emory University; after the children were born, she wrote at night, when she'd done the dishes.

One of her works was published in a small university quarterly, but it was not until 1962, when she was thirty-two, that she got her first check. Le Guin had given up reading science fiction years before, because all it seemed to be about was "hardware and soldiers." But a friend encouraged her to read Harlan Ellison, Philip K. Dick, and Theodore Sturgeon, and Le Guin discovered that the genre was changing. The first story she submitted to the science-fiction market was bought by a woman editor—Cele Goldsmith Lalli, then with *Fantastic* and *Amazing* magazines, both fantasy/sci-fi monthlies. For that story, "April in Paris," Le Guin got $30, which she immediately spent on a pair of brown wool pants she had seen advertised in the *New Yorker*.

She published four novels before *The Left Hand of Darkness*. Then, in 1970, she made of her hometown, Portland, a novel. *The Lathe of Heaven* is about a small, ordinary draftsman named George, who discovers that he

can change the future (and the past, retroactively) by his
dreams. It is a very delicate novel, populated by ordinary
people and turtlelike aliens who find themselves in the
midst of environmental catastrophes. Le Guin says she was
paying homage to the late Philip K. Dick, author of *Do
Androids Dream of Electric Sheep?* from which the movie
Blade Runner was made, badly in Le Guin's opinion. Dick's
books are filled with small businessmen going broke. One
gets by, advises an alien in *The Lathe of Heaven*, with a little
help from one's friends.

Portland is a small, easy city built along the banks of
the Williamette. It is a Le Guin city, as if parts of it had
been invented by her. There is Powell's Books, for example,
which inhabits an old car-dealership garage. In Powell's you
can find anything; you can mumble at the counter clerk
about that, ah, book about liberation theology and he'll re-
ply, "*Cry of the People*—downstairs, history." There's Jake's
(crawfish, Anchor Steam beer, old wooden booths) and,
down by the Williamette, there's Waterfront Park, with
an area dedicated to Francis J. Murnane, former president
of Local 8, ILWU. Near this park, every weekend, is the
Portland Saturday Market ("Rain or shine, April through
Christmas"), with crafts booths and food from teriyaki to
huge, flat pastries called elephant ears. When I visited the
park, four children with violins were playing a Branden-
burg concerto under a freeway bridge.

Portland has sensible building-height regulations—460
feet, or about fifty stories—and many parks, including one
downtown that has traditionally been reserved for women.

(In 1904, the women in Portland decided they wanted a place of their own. There used to be an elderly ombudsman who stood at the entrance to the women's park and gently advised men not to go in without an escort.) Over a drinking fountain near the public library is carved in stone, "Tongues in trees/Books in the running brooks/Sermons in stones/And good in everything." I stayed in a pleasant old hotel near downtown for $24 a night.

The Le Guins have lived near Forest Park for twenty-three years. (There tend to be a lot of trees in Le Guin's novels. She once called herself science fiction's "most arboreal writer.") When I went up to the park for a walk on Sunday morning, a couple sat on a bridge there drinking champagne out of martini glasses.

The Le Guins and I met downtown on the evening of August 6, near the women's park, for an artists' program in memory of the bombing of Hiroshima. The night before, two hundred people had painted two thousand "shadows" on the sidewalks of Portland, outlines, one of a man playing with a cat, as reminders of the way radiation from the Hiroshima bomb burned the forms of its victims onto the sides of buildings. Le Guin read a poem toward the end of the evening's program:

We lived forever until 1945.

Children have time to make mistakes,
margin for error. Carthage
could be destroyed and sown with salt.

Everything was always. It would be all right.
Then we turned
(so technically sweet the turning)
the light on.
In the desert of that dividing light we saw
the writing on the walls of the world.

Afterward, we walked down to Waterfront Park and people launched white balloons carrying paper cranes out over the river. A small group of drunk gentlemen stood off to the side of the demonstrators and sang something like, "The queers are dying, the queers are dying" over and over again, until someone in the crowd began to sing, very softly, "All we are saying is give peace a chance." And then another person picked it up, "All we are saying . . ." and then another—and soon, the drunken men were quiet and there was a great stillness over the water above the voices.

•   •   •

In 1974, Le Guin published her second novel to win both the Hugo and Nebula awards, *The Dispossessed: An Ambiguous Utopia*, which took her two and a half years to write and is her most explicit political statement to date.

In the several years prior to beginning the novel, Le Guin had been reading the major anarchist thinkers, among them Peter Kropotkin and Paul Goodman. Kropotkin was a nineteenth-century Russian natural scientist who, after observing animal and human life in Siberia and elsewhere in Russia, took on the Social Darwinists of his time in his book *Mutual Aid*. The point of *Mutual Aid* is that creatures of all kinds do not progress or survive by competing with one another, but instead cooperate to assure mutual survival. A very sweet-tempered, gentle man, Kropotkin was imprisoned in Russia (for conspiracy against the czar) in 1874, escaped to Western Europe and did not return to his homeland until the middle of the revolution in 1917. Although Kropotkin was supportive of the revolution, he became more and more critical of the Bolsheviks, finally breaking with Lenin entirely in 1920. He died, in despair, a year later.

Goodman was a twentieth-century American whose book on adolescent boys, *Growing up Absurd*, became a bestseller in the 1960s and is his best-known work. Like Kropotkin's, Goodman's thinking spanned many disciplines: he was a poet, a novelist, a lay therapist and a social critic. His early literary career suffered because he was a pacifist during World War II and an open homosexual. To most people, an anarchist is a bomb-throwing terrorist and anarchy means chaos. There have been violent anarchists, but much of anarchy's bad name comes from successful propaganda against it. Anarchy is a loosely organized but often very successful political philosophy. (The recent "affinity groups" used by nuclear protesters were invented by anarchists during the Spanish Civil War.) To put it simply: anarchy is based on the realistic observation that people left to themselves, without the intervention of the state, tend to cooperate and work out their differences. This process may be awkward, inefficient and punctuated by fights, but its end result is usually more satisfying to everyone than when things are done by command.

Anarchists tend to be less theoretical and more practical than most political ideologues, relying on observation to prove their points. Thus, Goodman wrote about seating arrangements, banning cars from Manhattan, why vacant lots are good for children, why snow should be allowed to pile up in cities during the winter so people can go sledding, and why freeways are bad for bicycles and roller skates. Goodman liked messy, active, human-scale cities. He often wrote about his belief that the work of human hands should be out in the open in our cities, not concealed in factories far from downtown. Kropotkin recorded how peasants fought fires together and dealt with childbirth.

For Le Guin, reading them and other anarchists was "like breathing fresh air. They talked about everyday life. How you do it. As a concrete thinker, as a housewife, in a number of ways, they were talking my language."

To show how anarchism might work, Le Guin constructed the planet Annares, an anarchist's utopia. A desert planet, it is a postindustrial world—there are trains, factories, even a computer—but there are no laws or money ("To make a thief, make an owner: to create crime, create laws"); no prisons, almost no personal property, no possessive pronouns.

For contrast, and to compare anarchism to capitalism, Le Guin made another planet, Urras, a bountiful, expensive, beautiful world, populated by gorgeously arrayed men and women (the women have magnets implanted under their skin to hold jewels in place) and the hidden poor. Each planet is the moon of the other.

The hero of *The Dispossessed* is Shevek, a physicist, partly modeled after J. Robert Oppenheimer. Born on Annares, he eventually travels to Urras. Through Shevek's eyes, we see the two planets. A city on Annares is Le Guin's tribute to Paul Goodman:

> He passed a glassworks, the workman dipping up a great molten blob as casually as a cook serves soup. Next to it was a busy yard where foamstone was cast for construction. The gang foreman, a big woman in a smock white with dust, was supervising the pouring of a cast with a loud and splendid flow of language. After that came a small wire factory, a district laundry, a luthier's where musical instruments were made and repaired, the district small-goods distributory, a theater, a tile works. The activity going on in each place was fascinating, and mostly out in full view. Children were around, some involved in the work with adults, some underfoot making mud-pies, some busy with games in the street, one sitting perched up on the roof of the learning center with her nose deep in a book . . . No doors were locked, few shut. There were no disguises and no advertisements. It was all there, all the

work, all the life of the city, open to the eye and
to the hand.

On a street on Urras, Shevek goes shopping for the
first time in his life:

Saemtenevia Prospect was two miles long, and
it was a solid mass of people, traffic, and things:
things to buy, things for sale. Coats, dresses,
gowns, robes, trousers, breeches, shirts, blouses,
hats, shoes, stockings, scarves, shawls, vests,
capes, umbrellas, clothes to wear while sleeping,
while swimming, while playing games, while at
an afternoon party, while at an evening party,
while at a party in the country, while traveling,
while at the theater, while riding horses, garden-
ing, receiving guests, boating, dining, hunting—
all different . . .

And the strangest thing about the nightmare
street was that none of the millions of things for
sale were made there. They were only sold there.
Where were the workshops, the factories, where
were the farmers, the craftsmen, the miners, the
weavers, the chemists, the carvers, the dyers, the
designers, the machinists, where were the hands,
the people who made? Out of sight, somewhere
else. Behind walls. All the people in all the shops
were either buyers or sellers. They had no relation
to the things but that of possession.

In an unusual move before she had completed the manuscript, Le Guin showed it to a friend, the Marxist critic Darko Suvin, who teaches at McGill University in Montreal. Le Guin believes that Marxists and anarchists are their own best critics, "the only people that seem to speak to each other's main problems." He told her, among other things, that she couldn't have twelve chapters in an anarchist book; she must have thirteen. And he told her that her ending was too tight, too complete. Le Guin added a chapter and made the book open-ended.

When *The Dispossessed* was finished, Le Guin was exhausted. "I sat around and was sure I never would write again. I read Jung and I consulted the *I Ching*. For eighteen months, it gave me the same answer: the wise fox sits still or something."

• • •

Since 1974, when *The Dispossessed* was published, Le Guin has published three short novels, a collection of essays and two collections of short stories. (*The Compass Rose*, the most recent, includes a story about the use of electric shock on political prisoners in a country very much like Chile.) Only one of her recent stories takes place in outer space.

"Space was a metaphor for me. A beautiful, lovely, endlessly rich metaphor for me," Le Guin says looking down toward the docks, "until it ended quite abruptly after *The*

Dispossessed. I had a loss of faith. I simply—I can't explain it. I don't seem to be able to do outer space anymore.

"The last outer-space story I did was in *The Compass Rose*. It's called 'The Pathways of Desire,' and it turns out to be a hoax in a sense. Apparently it's an expression of my loss of faith."

She hates the immensely popular science-fiction films of George Lucas and Steven Spielberg. "I wouldn't go to see *E.T.*, to tell you the truth, because I disliked *Close Encounters* so profoundly.

"It seems so exploitive. I don't know, his attitude toward people is so weird. At the end of *Close Encounters* she's got that beautiful little kid back, you know. He's been lost for weeks or months, hasn't he? She's got her little kid back—*what is she doing* taking photographs? She doesn't even have her arm around the kid. It bugs me."

She pauses and then goes on. "I feel a little weird about standing aside and being snooty because it does seem like they're not—you can't talk about them quite like ordinary movies or like an art form. It's almost like a ritual. People go because other people go. It's a connection thing, isn't it? It's a weird way for people to communicate. But the trouble is, in other words, in a sense it's like a religious communion, but it's so terribly low-grade, morally so cheap. *Star Wars* is really abominable: it's all violence, and there are only three women in the known universe.

"These films are working on a very low level intellectually and morally, and in their blindness perhaps they do get close to people's feelings," she continues, "because they are not only non-intellectual, they are anti-intellectual and sort of deliberately stupid. But I would rather say that about *Star Wars*. I think Steven Spielberg, on the other hand, is playing a very tricky game. I think he knows. I think he deliberately exploits archetypal images in a way that I really dislike a lot."

(I ask her how she got through dinner parties when everyone was carrying on about *E.T.* "I didn't say anything," she replies, and then changes her voice to a linebacker's—"I want to be loved.")

"I did follow our space flights. The little *Voyagers*? God, those were lovely. But what we are doing now I find in itself extremely depressing—the space shuttle. I'm not happy about it the way I was happy about the other ones. It's all military-industrial. It's a bunch of crap flying around the world, just garbage in the sky. I think that did have to do with my loss of faith. My God, we could muck that up just as bad as—we're going to repeat the same . . .

"I think we're sick," she finally says. "I hate to make big pronouncements, but I don't know how you bring up a kid. There's the size of our population and people who work so hard, and no one praises them for it. We've overbred our species."

But, I point out, the saving grace for us in many of her books is the presence of others.

"But they don't have to be human others," she replies. "We live with others on all sides at all times. That's the thing about religion, about monotheism. They say we're other and better. It's a very silly and dangerous course. It also relates to feminism. Women have been treated as animals have been. If the men insist on talking about it that way, then the men and God can walk in Eden—they can walk alone there."

   She gets up at 5:30 in the morning these days to work on the new book, in the little room at the end of the hall. The population in the book is very small, nearly that of the world in the late Stone Age, a few million here, a few million there, and great herds of animals. There is no hero in the book; there are many, many voices and a female anthropologist named Pandora.

·   ·   ·

Before I leave, we go out to Sauvie Island to pick blueberries. Finding none to pick, we picnic on the banks of the Columbia. Ursula asks Charles if it was Debbie Reynolds who divorced Eddie Fisher because he brushed his teeth with warm water, and Charles replies no, it was Elizabeth Taylor who divorced Nicky Hilton. She rolls up her pants and stands in the shallow water, the wake of the ships moving in neat waves toward her, each wave a pattern, each one the exact same distance from the next as they stroke the shore.

   Mozart heard his music all at once, she had told me earlier, then he had to write it down, to extend it into time.

DRIVEN BY A DIFFERENT CHAUFFEUR

INTERVIEW BY NICK GEVERS
SF SITE
NOVEMBER/DECEMBER 2001

Ursula K. Le Guin wears many creative hats: as poet, essayist, translator, writer for young children, illustrator, mainstream literary author; but it is surely in her fantasy and science fiction that her especial genius resides. Her two great series, the Earthsea and Ekumenical tales, are ample evidence of that. Earthsea is a many-isled realm of composed and chthonic magics, of dragons and wizards, of frail arrogance and vast humility. The Ekumenical or Hainish Cycle is complex SF, rich in utopian surmise and anthropological reflection. As her recent work is largely preoccupied with matters of Ekumen and Earthsea, it is there that the emphasis of this interview naturally falls.

I interviewed Le Guin by letter in November and December of 2001, in anticipation of the publication of her major new collection, *The Birthday of the World and Other Stories*, in March 2002. Le Guin is a subtly but firmly opinionated writer, and I posed her some deliberately provocative questions. She responded with all the vigor I hoped for, pouncing on many of my stated assumptions with the kindly didacticism for which she is famed. So: if some of the questions below seem naïve or crass, please remember, reader, that they were sacrificial in nature, and for all that, many people would agree heartily with their premises. Le Guin's fictions are engines of thought, and much of that thought must run contrary to hers.

NICK GEVERS: *The Telling, Tales from Earthsea, The Other Wind*, and *The Birthday of the World and Other Stories*: four major new books in under two years, including your first novels since *Tehanu*; probably your most prolific period since the 1970s. To what would you ascribe this productivity?

URSULA K. LE GUIN: This effect of immense industriousness is an artifact of the peculiarities of the publishing industry. I was writing along at about my usual rate for some years without being sure where to publish in book form (for various reasons—changes of editors, of literary agents, etc.). My new publisher, Harcourt, once they got onto me, were eager to print everything I gave them in very short order; and then my old publisher, Harper, suddenly decided I was still alive. So I end up with four books in two years (five, counting a long-delayed kid's book, *Tom Mouse*, to come out in March).

Two of these new books assemble stories I wrote in the 1990s but didn't include in my 1990s collections *A Fisherman of the Inland Sea, Unlocking the Air, Searoad*, and *Four Ways to Forgiveness*. (Those last two, being story-suites, count, in my mind, pretty much the same as novels. Similarly, *Tales from Earthsea* isn't a novel, but it carries the Earthsea series from *Tehanu* to *The Other Wind* without a break.) Then the two novels, *The Telling* and *The Other Wind*, came one right after the other at the end of the decade. One came slow, the other fast.

GEVERS: The hallmark of your work over the last decade has been a return to, a revisioning of, your original Hainish and Earthsea sequences. One should never speak too soon, but do you think you've now finished with Earthsea and the Ekumen, rounded them off conclusively?

LE GUIN: Earthsea got revisited and revisioned, and certain obscurities were made clear. The Ekumen worlds merely got further explored, it seems to me.

I don't know that I've finished anything. Certainly not the Ekumen, which has no shape and, therefore, no end.

I seem to tend to avoid conclusive conclusions, as it were, she said, evasively and inconclusively. I like to leave doors open.

GEVERS: Your newest works have a strong reconciliatory air: not a compromise with patriarchy and tyranny, but a bringing together of masculine and feminine elements that seemed mutually alienated in your middle-period works like *Always Coming Home* and *Tehanu*. Have you mellowed? Or has your ideological emphasis simply shifted?

LE GUIN: Thank you; I like "reconciliatory not compromising."

But I wonder why you find masculine and feminine elements "alienated" in *Tehanu* and not in *A Wizard of Earthsea* and *The Farthest Shore*, books which have no female characters of any importance. Absence is not alienation?

Tehanu is the beginning of a genuine reconciliation. The first steps are the hard ones.

As for the masculine and feminine elements in *Always Coming Home*, my own opinion is that it's in that book, of all my works, that the reunion, cooperation, harmony of the genders (among the Kesh) reach perhaps the highest degree. Of course, this would not be visible to people who perceive gender harmony only as a result of either one being superior to or dominating the other. Such people insist on describing Kesh society as "matriarchal," which is nonsense. Apparently their logic is: if it isn't patriarchal, it has to be matriarchal. Hierarchism dies very hard, doesn't it?

As for mellowing, I'd like to be good-natured and open-minded, but certainly do not want to mellow into mere mushiness. Like pears that rot from the inside. I'd rather be like Cabernet. Except that would involve staying bottled up for years . . .

As for ideology, the hell with it. All of it.

GEVERS: In line with the previous question: your style has shifted with time, from a rich mythic/epic register early on to the spare, precisely honed diction of your 1980s work. Now, the two seem to combine, alternating or mingling in a stylistic reconciliation. How deliberate is this fusion?

LE GUIN: Nothing I do is exactly deliberate.

But I do work very hard and consciously at my craft. At the sound, the flow, the exactness, the connections, the implications of my words.

GEVERS: A striking contrast between the original Earthsea and Ekumen novels and their recent successors is the latter's move from action to observation: *The Telling* and *The Other Wind* are contemplative and discursive rather than plot-driven. Why is this?

LE GUIN: Probably because I was getting into my seventies when I wrote them. There is something about one's body as it gets around seventy years old that induces—strongly—often imperatively—a shift from action to observation. Action at seventy tends to lead to a lot of saying *ow, ow, ow.* Observation, however, can be rewarding. As I never have been sure where my body leaves off and my mind begins or vice-versa, it seems unsurprising to me that the condition of one of them induces a similar condition in the other.

Anyhow, I have never written a plot-driven novel. I admire plot from a vast distance, with unenvious admiration. I don't do it; never did it; don't want to; can't. My stories are driven (rather slowly and erratically, with pauses to admire apparently irrelevant scenery) by a different chauffeur.

GEVERS: Ever since *Always Coming Home*, you've seemed to advocate a profound simplicity of life-style: communal, agrarian, sustainable. The Kesh of *Always* live that way, and then there are the folk of the planet O in various stories, Ged in his goat-tending and turnip-cultivating retirement on Gont, et cetera. But isn't this idea sentimentally nostalgic, and, in the wrong hands (Pol Pot) positively dangerous?

LE GUIN: Could we have this question again? There is a genuine problem in it, but in its present form I cannot answer it; it seems to either answer itself or destroy itself. The terms are ideological and self-contradictory. A "sustainable" lifestyle is "sentimentally nostalgic"?

A man in a non-industrial economy, who no longer has a source of income, but does have the use of a small piece of land, tends goats and (I'm sorry, I do not recollect any turnips in Earthsea) a kitchen garden, poultry, fruit trees. What else would you suggest that he do, if he likes to eat now and then?*

Of course the mere idea of the existence of a non-industrial economy may be what you are considering as "sentimentally nostalgic."

The question of nostalgia deserves looking into. Much fantasy, and science fiction too, draws upon an apparently inalterable human longing for "the peaceable kingdom," the garden Voltaire suggested we cultivate. But terms must be used carefully and respectfully in such a discussion.

Any refusal to accept the abuse of the world by ill-considered, misapplied technologies as desirable/inevitable can be labelled Luddite. All genuine alternatives to Industrial Capitalism can be, and are, dismissed as "nostalgia."

All ideals are positively dangerous. All idealists are dangerous: Pol Pot, Jean-Jacques Rousseau, Jefferson, Lenin, Osama Bin Laden, Francis of Assisi.

What is endangered, and how it is endangered may, however, vary.

---

* The turnips were rhetorical—Nick Gevers

And there may be a difference—a subtle one, a crucial one—between idealists and ideologues.

GEVERS: The fate of Earth in the Ekumen series is not exactly apocalyptic, but quite bleak, blighted, and theocratic, as hinted in *The Dispossessed* and shown in more detail in the story "Dancing to Ganam" and *The Telling*. How close is this portrait to your actual expectations for the planet?

LE GUIN: I don't know. Sometimes I think I am just trying superstitiously to avert evil by talking about it; I certainly don't consider my fictions prophetic. Yet throughout my whole adult life, I have watched us blighting our world irrevocably, irremediably, and mindlessly—ignoring every warning and neglecting every benevolent alternative in the pursuit of "growth" and immediate profit. It is quite hard to live in the United States in 2001 and feel any long term hopefulness about the unrelenting use of increasingly exploitative and destructive technologies: not so much weaponry, at this point, as technologies that could and should be useful and productive—fuel sources, agriculture, genetic engineering, even medicine. And, of course, we keep breeding.

Dark visions of a theocratic world have been fueled by the rise, during the last two or three decades, of the fundamentalist side of every world religion, and the willingness of many people to believe that fundamentalism is religion.

I might point out that the unhappy Earth hinted at in some of the Ekumenical fictions would be only a dark passage on the way to the very far future Earth of my most hopeful book, *Always Coming Home*. Believing that we have no future but that of high-tech development, urgent expansion, urbanization, and ruthless exploitation of natural and human resources—believing that we have to go on as we are going now—people tend to see that book as backward-turning. It isn't. It looks at, but not back. It's a radical attempt to think outside current assumptions, a refusal of them. It's an attempt to portray a genuinely mature society. To imagine a "climax technology," the principle of which would not be enforced growth, but homeostasis. To offer not a mechanical but an organic model for culture.

GEVERS: *The Telling* could be read as a science-fictional allegory of the plight of the Tibetans under Chinese rule, or more broadly of the suppression of traditional wisdom under Communism of a corporatist sort, as in China as a whole. Does this mean that such traditional wisdom (theocratic in nature in Tibet) is infallible, or exempt from criticism in its turn?

LE GUIN: Actually, it was not Tibetan Buddhism, but what happened to the practice and teaching of Taoism under Mao that was the initial impetus of the book. I was shocked to find that a twenty-five-hundred-year-old body of thought, belief, ritual, and art could be, had been, essentially destroyed within ten years, and shocked to find I hadn't known it, though it happened during my adult lifetime. The atrocity, and my long ignorance of it, haunted me. I had to write about it, in my own sidelong fashion.

I don't know why you ask if I "mean" that any traditional wisdom, or any theocracy, is infallible or exempt from criticism. *The Telling* is indeed shown as a flexible and rather amiable tradition, very attractive to our point-of-view character; but she and I and they leave infallibility to popes. *The Telling* has no clergy, even: only people who take on ritual function at certain times. The tradition has no god, gods, hierarchical worship, or prayer. Because she is in the process of discovering it little by little, and because it is a badly damaged, currently illegal tradition, barely clinging to existence, Sutty has no basis from which to criticize it, and no particular reason to do so. But she does remain on the look-out for religiosity of the kind she knew on Earth, which she detests and distrusts with all her heart. Surely the novel does not show the Unist theocracy governing Earth as wise, infallible, or above criticism?

Your question sounds as if you kept thinking "Tibetan Buddhism," and did not believe what I was telling you in the book. An example of why the practice of "telling" takes quite a lot of practice . . . as it implies listening . . .

GEVERS: *The Other Wind* completes a retraction or renunciation, begun in *Tehanu* and *Tales from Earthsea*, of the premises of the original *Earthsea* trilogy: magic itself is invalidated to a great degree. How do you intend the first three books to be read now? In their spontaneous, shall we say, majesty, or with the qualification of hindsight?

LE GUIN: Well, Nick, and when did you stop beating your wife?

The assumptions stated in the first sentence of this question are simply wrong, which means that I can't answer but can only retort with questions.

Why do you say magic is invalidated in the last three Earthsea books? On what evidence? Because Ged can't do it anymore—one man, who gave up his power knowing what he was doing and why? Has the School on Roke closed? Have the Old Powers died? Are the dragons grounded? Is the Patterner not still in his Grove, and is the Grove not the still and ever-moving center of the world?

I will not say how I "intend" the books to be read; I have and want no control over my readers, except, of course, the sway of the stories themselves. Different people will read my trilogies different ways and that's as it should be. Because the first trilogy is more accessible to kids, they may stop with it, and then come back when they grow up, and go on with the second set.

But if the second trilogy invalidated, or retracted, or revoked the first one, I wouldn't have written it.

The second trilogy enlarges the first, which is very strong but narrow, leaving out far too much of the world.

The second trilogy changes nothing in the first. It sees exactly the same world with different eyes. Almost, I would say, with two eyes, rather than one.

All the books are, in large part, fictional studies of power. The first three see power mostly from the point of view of the powerful. The second three see power from the point of view of people who have none, or have lost it, or who can see their power as one of the illusions of mortality.

GEVERS: Looking now at the stories in *The Birthday of the World*: "Old Music and the Slave Women" is a continuation of the Werel novella cycle already published [in 1995] as *Four Ways to Forgiveness*. Is "Old Music" a similarly patterned fifth way to forgiveness, or does it differ in its essence from the earlier Werel/Yeowe tales?

LE GUIN: Thank you for talking about new and recent work. So many people don't, and I do get weary of answering questions about novels I wrote thirty years ago! Of course, I have developed nice glib answers to the more inevitable questions about them, while I may stammer a bit about the more recent works. "Old Music and the Slave Women" is a fifth way to forgiveness that didn't get itself written in time to get into the book. It is, however, a bit bleaker than the first four. (See above re: Idealists.) It is a mourning for the horrors of war. Old wars, new wars. Goya's wars. Our wars.

By the way, I have finally come up with a name for books like *Four Ways* and *Searoad*—stories that are genuinely connected by place and/or theme and/or characters. Such a book is a story suite, on the analogy of Bach's cello suites. The story suite is a common enough form, particularly in science fiction, that I wish (dream on!) could be recognized as such—not labeled and dismissed as a collection, certainly not as a "fix-up," but seen as a genuine fictional form in its own right, conceived as such not patched together, and with its own intriguing and complex aesthetic.

GEVERS: "Coming of Age in Karhide" is an unexpectedly direct return to the setting of *The Left Hand of Darkness*. Is it a sequel to that famous novel, or more of an anthropological footnote to it?

LE GUIN: Well, a short story can't be a sequel to a novel, but it can follow from it (sequitur)—no? If it's a footnote, I wouldn't call it so much anthropological as sexual. It seemed high time we got all the way into a kemmerhouse. With a native guide, instead of a poor uptight Earth guy trying to figure out what's going on and being disturbed by it . . . *Left Hand* gives the reader very little opportunity to experience being double-gendered, since Estraven is mostly in somer; there's only a brief, though crucial, scene involving kemmer, and most of that is from Genly's POV. I wanted to explore it as a natural, universal experience, instead of a weird alien condition. Back in 1968, I and most readers needed Genly Ai's POV to mediate the strangeness. I don't think we do, now. *(Si muove lente, eppur si muove!)*

GEVERS: "The Matter of Seggri" is perhaps the most experimental of your late Hainish tales, a particularly radical and affecting take on gender relations. What inspired its male-scarcity scenario, and your decision to employ such a multiplicity of narrative voices?

LE GUIN: I kept reading about how many female fetuses were being aborted in India, China, and other societies where the only baby worth having is a male, and about the future surplus of men and deficit of women if the trend continues. My bent imagination bent this whole scenario around and produced a great surplus of women, which biologically speaking is of course far more practical, but humanly speaking . . . ? Well, that is where the imagination actually gets to work. Producing a story. A set of stories. As many stories as there are people . . . Hence, perhaps, the variety of voices.

Many of my works since the 1980s have used multiple narrative voices in various ways. I often find this multiplicity an essential tool to storytelling at this point. Also, it can lead, paradoxically, to brevity; and I'm very fond of the novella length. There is certainly material enough for a novel in "Seggri," but I liked keeping it short, allusive, suggestive. Have had enough of novels where one voice yatters on and on . . .

GEVERS: The O stories—"Mountain Ways" and "Unchosen Love"—are (like the earlier "Another Story") set in a society divided into two elaborate moieties and practicing a profoundly cumbersome marital system. Would such a four-person hetero- and homosexual menage be practical? Or is this "sedoretu" system a thought experiment, a satiric or parodic construct?

LE GUIN: Well, writing the stories, I thought of the

sedoretu as pure thought-experiment—a highly enjoyable
tool for exploring human relations and emotions. I hadn't
exactly thought of it as satirical. We are so good at making
life difficult for ourselves, not least by inventing almost
impossible customs. Monogamous lifelong heterosexual
marriage is such a peculiar institution that it hardly seems
to need to be made fun of. But of course if you make marriage even harder than it is, involving four people instead
of two, and homosexuality as well as heterosexuality, it
gets even more interesting. At least, it does to me. But I
find all cumbersome cultural constructs and customs interesting. I am an anthropologist's daughter, after all.

You ask if the sedoretu would be practical. I don't
know. Is monogamous heterosexual marriage practical? I
don't know. My husband and I have done it for forty-eight
years, but that could just be luck, and a bit of practice.

GEVERS: "The Birthday of the World": is this a retelling
of sorts of the Spanish conquest of Peru? Does the story
form part of the Hainish Cycle?

LE GUIN: Certain aspects of the society in the story were
borrowed from Incan Peru, and the absoluteness and sud-
denness of the social collapse resemble what happened
to the Incan Empire when the Spanish came, but it's not
meant to be a commentary in any way on that society and
that event. I guess it's partly a meditation on the also note-
worthy fragility of our cultural constructs. Whether it's
an Ekumenical story I honestly don't know. It could be.

GEVERS: Who, for you, are the finest SF authors now writing—both your fellow feminist writers and more generally?

LE GUIN: First I am to list fellow feminists and then . . . non-fellow anti-feminists? Come on, Nick, let's get out of the pigeonholes. If feminism is the idea that differences between the genders, beyond the strictly physiological, are an interesting subject of study, but have not been determined, and so are not a sound basis for society to use in prescribing or proscribing any proclivity or activity—which is what I think it is—then I probably don't read any non-feminist SF writers, these days. Do you? Anyhow, I hate trying to answer this who-do-you-like-best question, because I always leave out people I meant to mention, and then kick myself later. Allow me to dodge this one, okay?

GEVERS: You've been writing fascinating "Interplanary" sociological portraits for a while now. When do you expect to assemble these into *Changing Planes*? And what other projects lie on the horizon?

LE GUIN: Thank you for asking, and for calling those stories fascinating. I have been afraid people might find them infuriating. They certainly exemplify my fine disregard for plot. Perhaps they will puzzle some of my critics, who treat my work as if it had all the comic possibilities of a lead ingot. Anyhow, the manuscript is out; it is in the hands of the agents, the publishers, the editors, the

Fates, the Furies, whoever. I hope there will be a book of *Changing Planes*.

But changing planes isn't quite what it was before the eleventh of September of this year, is it?

At the moment I am working hard to complete a translation of a fairly large portion of the poetry of the Chilean poet Gabriela Mistral. After that, *quien sabe?*

SONG OF HERSELF

INTERVIEW BY BRIDGET HUBER
CALIFORNIA MAGAZINE
SPRING 2013

Ursula K. Le Guin has said that her father, Alfred Kroeber, studied real cultures, while she made them up. Indeed, many of the writer's most celebrated novels are set in intricately imagined realms, from the sci-fi universe of Ekumen to the fantasy archipelago of Earthsea.

This inventor of worlds grew up in Berkeley. Her father was the University of California's first professor of anthropology. Kroeber Hall, the campus building that houses the department, is named in his honor. A pioneer of cultural anthropology, today Professor Kroeber is best remembered for his association with and research on Ishi, the man believed at the time to have been the last of the California Yahi tribe. He was even called "the last wild Indian in North America."

That was the subtitle, in fact, of the book *Ishi in Two Worlds*, written by Le Guin's mother, Theodora Kroeber, who met Le Guin's father while she was a graduate student at Berkeley. The book made her famous in her own right. Now in a fiftieth anniversary edition from UC Press, *Ishi in Two Worlds* has sold more than one million copies.

Le Guin and her three older brothers grew up in a Bernard Maybeck house on Arch Street, not far from campus. She remembers life there as "easygoing and generous" and that the family home was filled with the conversation of "interesting grown-ups"—including academics, intellectuals and the members of various California Indian tribes.

California Magazine caught up with Le Guin as she was preparing to come to the Berkeley campus to deliver the 2013 Avenali Lecture. The event, sponsored by the Townsend Center for the Humanities, was entitled "What Can Novels Do? A Conversation with Ursula Le Guin."

What follows is an edited transcript of our own conversation with the Berkeley native about being a child, a mother, and a grandmother—in short, about growing up and growing old.

BRIDGET HUBER: Does a return to Berkeley bring back a flood of memories?

URSULA K. LE GUIN: I grew up in the 1930s and '40s, and Berkeley was a rather small city then. It didn't have the reputation that it got later of being extremely leftist, liberal, independent. It was just kind of a more conventional university town. It was an extremely nice place to be a kid. I could go anywhere. My best friend and I, we played all over the campus, and the campus wasn't all built up yet, you know? There were lots of lawns and forests, and Strawberry Creek was like a little wild creek. It was a wonderful place to play.

HUBER: Wasn't Berkeley somewhat bohemian even back then?

LE GUIN: There was room for bohemians in it, but it was really pretty middle class. Not rigidly middle-class like you might get in the Midwest; there was a lot of latitude always in Berkeley, and in the thirties and forties of course it was full of refugees from Europe because the university had a wonderful policy of taking in intellectuals who were running from Hitler or Mussolini. I do believe that influx of brilliant European minds may have stirred the city up a bit.

HUBER: How would you characterize your parents' parenting style? How did they raise you?

LE GUIN: Well, I think they did a real good job. [*Laughs*] They were very loving and very patient, but they didn't hover. I wasn't very rebellious because there wasn't anything to rebel against. It was kind of easy to be a good girl. And I had three big brothers, and that was kind of cool, too.

HUBER: Were you children part of the dinner table conversations at home?

LE GUIN: As soon as we got old enough. I think until we were about five we'd eat upstairs with my great-aunt Betsy, who lived with us. I think from about five on we were considered civilized. Then Betsy got to come downstairs with us. [*Laughs*] We were all there at dinner, and there was always conversation at dinner. In that sense, it probably seems very old-fashioned to people now.

HUBER: I was struck by your description of the teenage summers you spent at your family's ranch, wandering the hills alone. You said about it, "I think I started making my soul then." Why are experiences like that important for kids to have?

LE GUIN: It does seem that, in the last twenty years or so, children get extraordinarily little solitude. Things are provided to do at all times, and the homework is so much heavier than what we had. But the solitude, the big empty day with nothing in it where you have to kind of make your day yourself, I do think that's very important for kids growing up. I'm not talking about loneliness. I'm talking about having the option of being alone.

If you're a very extroverted person, you probably don't want that. But if you're on the introverted side, you're not given much room in the world we've got now. You're kind of driven into this whole sociability of the social media. Texting is wonderful for teenagers. I was on the telephone all the time when I was thirteen, with my best friend. *Gabble gabble gabble gabble.* I mean, what do teenagers talk about? I don't know, but they need to do it. Texting looks like a wonderful way to do that, to just be in touch with each other all the time. But I think it's important that there also be the option not to be in touch for awhile, to just drop out. How do you know who you are if you're always with other people doing what they do? That's true all through life; it's not just kids.

HUBER: So you would argue that we should try to give kids more space.

LE GUIN: Yeah, give them some room. Give them room to be themselves, to flail around and make mistakes. I had lots of room given me, so at least I know enough to value it.

HUBER: Did your parents encourage you to write?

LE GUIN: Not exactly, they just saw I was doing it and they would say, "Hey, that's fine. Go ahead." But I was left very, very free. I had encouragement, but no pushing.

HUBER: Much has been made of the connection between your father's profession as an anthropologist and the nature of your fiction. How do you think his work influenced yours?

LE GUIN: I'm not sure that his work influenced mine, because I didn't really know his work until I was well into my twenties and thirties and began reading him. But I was formed as a writer earlier than that, to a large extent. My father and I had certain similarities, intellectually and temperamentally. We're interested in small details, in getting them right. We're interested in how people do things and what things they do and how they explain doing them. This is all kind of anthropological information. It's also novel information. It's what you build novels out of: human relationships, how people arrange their relationships. Anthropology and fiction, they overlap to a surprising extent.

HUBER: Was Ishi's story a big part of your consciousness growing up?

LE GUIN: No, I honestly knew nothing at all about Ishi until they asked my father to write about him and he sort of gave the job to my mother, and then she began researching him. This was in the very late fifties. Ishi died in 1916. I wasn't even born until 1929. My mother never knew Ishi. It was something way back in my father's life, and it was not a happy memory, I think, because of the way it ended. No. He had to feel very bad about the fact that Ishi died of white man's TB. My father did not reminisce. He wasn't one of those people who talked about old times. But I think there was some pain there that he didn't want to go back to. He was out of the country when Ishi died, and that always—they were friends, after all. That's always hard, to feel like, "I let him down." This is just guesswork on my part. He didn't want to talk about it, and it's not the kind of thing I would've asked him.

HUBER: What do you think about the way that Ishi was treated, and his relationship with your father?

LE GUIN: That's two different questions. One, the relationship was, as I can understand it, a deep friendship within this curious constraint of their sort of formal relationship. Ishi was an informant and an employee of the museum, and my father was a professor. It was a more formal age, remember. The general question of how it was handled . . . I have to say, I think they did about the best they could in the circumstances. They got Ishi a job. He had work to do within this white world that he'd been dumped into. And a place to live, which apparently he liked, and he could meet the public and try to show them what being a Yahi was. I realize it has come in for enormous criticism from generations who have a lot of hindsight and say, "My goodness, they were exploiting him, and they could have done it different," and so on, but they never convinced me that anybody then knew how to do it any better than they did. But it is a heartbreaking story.

HUBER: Your mother started writing late in life.

LE GUIN: She started writing about the same time I did, professionally speaking. She got published first. And of course she got a bestseller—*Ishi* was UC Press's first bestseller. She said, "Oh, I always wanted to write, but I didn't want it to compete with bringing up the kids, so I had to get you all out from under." That's how she felt. And once she started writing, I think she wrote most every day. She loved doing it. Both my parents wrote every day. I don't; I'm lazier. [*Laughs*]

HUBER: Your mother sounds like a very feisty and

independent, unconventional woman, especially for her era. How did she shape the kind of woman you became?

LE GUIN: It's so complicated. My mother didn't call herself a feminist, but she gave me Virginia Woolf's *A Room of One's Own* and *Three Guineas* to read when I was fourteen maybe. Those are very powerful books to give a girl. My mother was a freethinking person. She thought for herself. She read and thought and talked, she was intellectual, so I think what my mother gave me was just the example of a woman with a free mind who chose to be a wife, mother, housewife, a hostess—the conventional life of a middle-class woman. She liked it, very much. If she hadn't, I don't think she would have done it. Her mother was a very independent Wyoming woman. My great-aunt was a strong influence on me, and she was very much an independent Western woman who went her own way. That side of my family, they were strong Western women. There was a lot of independence there.

HUBER: Where do you think that your feminist consciousness came from, then?

LE GUIN: In my generation, it was beginning to grow everywhere, and I was even kind of slow catching up to the early feminist movement. But there came a point in our lives when it was kind of a matter of survival. Again, it's so complicated, but there has been a very large revolution in thinking during my lifetime. I think we won't go back to where we were when I was born, which was a man's world. And, you're talking to a writer here. Literature was so much a man's world. And it still is. Look at who the prizes go to. It's a very slow revolution, and it doesn't involve blood and killing people and burning bras and all that stuff. It's just, it's going to happen. It's happening.

HUBER: You have written about the way that you balanced your writing career with raising your three children, and it sounds like . . .

LE GUIN: To call it a balance . . . It seemed kind of like a madhouse sometimes.

HUBER: How did you and your husband share this work of childrearing?

LE GUIN: That was really the secret, that I had this guy who could do his job and let me do my job, and then we did our job together, which was bring up the kids. And keeping a house—like my mother, I enjoy it. I don't think I kept the house very well, but I could keep things going and write.

HUBER: And so, when your children were small, would you write at night?

LE GUIN: Yeah, that's kind of all you can do. If you're home with the kids, you've got to be on duty. Unless you have servants or something.

HUBER: I want to ask you about a particular poem in *Finding My Elegy*, "Song for a Daughter." It begins:

> *Mother of my granddaughter,*
> *listen to my song:*
> *A mother can't do right,*
> *a daughter can't be wrong.*

Could you just tell me about what inspired that poem?

LE GUIN: What's going on in that poem? Well, when your daughter has a daughter, and her daughter's giving her trouble, you think, "Oh, boy." It's a wheel going around. And the way you feel about an angry four-year-old: You want to wring their neck, and you love them very much . . . and just kind of watching the generations repeat the pain and the love that we give each other, and the fact that the kid never can do anything right, and they also never can do anything wrong. That's the way it came out in my head. So that is a grandmother poem. It's got three generations going, and of course it involves my mother, and how I'm sure she felt sometimes, that I never could do anything right. But she never said so. She let me feel that I was doing okay.

HUBER: Do you feel more or less hopeful about the future now than you were when you began your writing career?

LE GUIN: Old age does not tend to make you very hopeful. It's not a hopeful time of life. Youth is. It has to be. And old age—you have seen enough things go to ruin that it gets a little harder to be hopeful. And when you're watching your species destroy their habitat, as we are doing, it is quite a job to remain hopeful. But then I also have realized, like we were talking about these huge social changes in gender and the relative positions of men and women. The changes are painfully slow, but they have happened, and they are continuing to happen. So there's hope.

HUBER: What are you working on now?

LE GUIN: I'm not writing much fiction now. I published one story this year, I think. Mostly doing poetry, and I do enjoy writing a blog on my website, which is kind of a new idea for me. There's a lot to keep up with, and at my age, I haven't got the energy I had, so I can't do as much as I used to. I do regret that, but that's just life.

HUBER: What do you like about writing a blog?

LE GUIN: I got the idea of doing it from the Portuguese Nobel Prize–winner, José Saramago. When he was eighty-five and eighty-six, he was writing blogs. And they're wonderful. Some of them are political and some of them are just kind of thoughtful. And I thought, "Well, wow. It's a very short form, and it's very free. Maybe I could do that." A blog can be anything you want it to be, so it's good for this condition I'm in of not having the energy to write a novel. You need a lot of strength to write a novel, honestly. It's a huge

job. And even a short story takes a kind of a big surge of
energy, and in your eighties, you tend to just kind of run
out of that stuff. It just isn't there anymore. So you parlay
what you've got. And then there's poetry, which is always a
blessing. And I've written poetry all my life, so I'm glad it's
still with me.

HUBER: Have you ever thought about writing a memoir?

LE GUIN: Memoir? No. I'm like my father: I'm not interested in talking about who I was. I'm much more interested
in finding out who I am. [*Laughs*] Going ahead.

THE LAST
INTERVIEW

HOMEWARD BOUND
INTERVIEW BY DAVID STREITFELD
2015–2018

Ursula K. Le Guin lived in exactly the kind of Portland neighborhood you would expect. There were marvelous coffeehouses, a library, the offices of a literary magazine, a self-consciously weird shop called The Peculiarium, a grocery co-op, friendly bars, and affordable restaurants—all the comforts of civilization presented at human scale. Le Guin's street started at the river, traversed the commercial center, rose sharply past a sign warning NO OUTLET, and crossed a gorge too deep for trolls before arriving at her house. Built in 1899, it felt bigger inside than it looked on the outside. The forest was only steps away, the largest urban wilderness in the country. I would smell the roses, take heed of the hand-printed sign imploring PLEASE DON'T LET THE CAT OUT!!, knock on the lion's-head door knocker, and be granted admission to the living room. The neat shelves held a complete set of Dickens, her beloved Calvino's *Cosmicomics*, an oversize tome titled *Beyond Time and Space*, and an Ovid with four hundred years of student scribbles. The walls displayed landscapes instead of award citations. The windows showed landscapes too—the Willamette River and then beyond to Mount St. Helens. It was a well-ordered but somewhat austere room, with polished wooden floors, beams of morning light, and no technology beyond the lamps.

Beginning in the summer of 2015, I sat in that room with Le Guin five times. We were planning a sixth meeting when a final illness took her at the beginning of 2018. The format was always the same: we placed ourselves in armchairs, separated by the width of the fireplace. The insults of age meant she could only sit still for an hour, and I tried hard never to exceed that limit. I always brought with me copies of her books, for quoting or reference. The early ones had garish and sometimes beautiful pulp covers. Le Guin chuckled frequently—the world amused her—but did not spare me when she felt I misunderstood something.

Pard, the black-and-white cat whose antics Le Guin chronicled on her blog, would stalk imperiously through. Charles, the writer's husband of six decades, was always home but never visible. "He's very shy," she explained. "He doesn't like to engage with 'my people,' as he calls them. He has his own people." In the evenings, she and Charles used these chairs to read to each other. Charles would read poetry first (once when I was there it was Theodore Roethke) and then Le Guin would do the prose (Richard Henry Dana's sea-faring epic *Two Years Before the Mast*). She would have a glass of mellow Speyside whisky. Charles, who hails from Georgia, would drink bourbon.

Extracts from our conversations appeared in *The New York Times* and the *Los Angeles Review of Books*. In advance of publication, she would sometimes revise a quote or expand it. Occasionally she softened a point about someone whom she scorned, like her fellow Library of America honoree, Philip Roth. In what follows, I went back to the original tapes to produce a definite record of our conversation, divided for the sake of clarity into two parts.

PART ONE

DAVID STREITFELD: I was perusing the bookcases here, and I didn't see any of your books.

URSULA K. LE GUIN: They fill the shelves of two bedrooms upstairs, one copy of each edition. So many different editions. [*Laughs*] I've had two partial bibliographies done of my work, but the last one was years ago. I was required to list the number of titles recently. I was told it was forty-seven. And I said, I'll bet there's more than that. I went through the bibliography on my website, which is just the main titles, no chapbooks. There were sixty, more than I realized. I can't keep up.

STREITFELD: I can't either. I know your work well but I was reading the other night a piece I hadn't read before, which I guess was performance art from the early 1990s. It was about being a woman who was really a man—because you were born before men acknowledged there were indeed such things as women. It was also about getting older and, among other things, Ernest Hemingway, he of "the beard and the guns and the wives and the little short sentences." It is deliciously unhinged:

Hemingway would have died rather than get

old. And he did. He shot himself. A short sentence. Anything rather than a long sentence, a life sentence. Death sentences are short and very, very manly. Life sentences aren't. They go on and on, all full of syntax and qualifying clauses and confusing references and getting old. And that brings up the real proof of what a mess I have made of being a man: I am not even young. Just about the time they finally started inventing women, I started getting old. And I went right on doing it. Shamelessly. I have allowed myself to get old and haven't done one single thing about it, with a gun or anything.*

LE GUIN: [*Laughs*] I was in a state when I wrote that. My early sixties, I guess. Now I'm even older. Much older. And I still don't have a gun.

STREITFELD: How does getting old look now?

LE GUIN: It's not the metaphysical weariness of aging that bothers me. It's that you get so goddamn physically tired you can't pull yourself together. If you've ever been very ill, it's like that. You just can't rise to the occasion. It's why I don't do many public appearances anymore. I'm a ham. I love appearing in front of an audience. But I can't.

STREITFELD: Even as a younger writer, you captured the

---

* "Introducing Myself." Appearing in *Left Bank*, archived at https://www.scholarsonline .org/~godsflunky/LeGuin_Intr_myself.pdf.

old. As I rapidly age myself, I keep returning to the story "The Day Before the Revolution." The heroine, Odo, has trouble moving and has trouble thinking.

LE GUIN: Old age is when you realize you can't do what you used to do. I know more about being older now and I feel compelled to write about it. Partly because there aren't very many old people in fiction, and they are just as interesting as younger people. And also, I think a writer who is still writing in her mid-eighties, like José Saramago or me—even if I'm only writing poetry—has a certain duty to report from the front. We are bearing witness to a place most people haven't been. You're how old? FIfty-four, fifty-six? Believe me, you haven't been there. You may think you're getting old, but you have a ways to go.

STREITFELD: It's a long slide downhill, it seems like.

LE GUIN: A long way to go doesn't tell you up or down, does it? It's just a long way to go. I'm neither an optimist nor a pessimist. I just tell it the way it is. [*Laughs*] Being an artist takes a certain amount of arrogance.

STREITFELD: With fiction writers, we expect them to go on forever. No one expects a surgeon to be operating on people when he's ninety-three. But the readers always want more.

LE GUIN: There was considerable amazement that Saramago was still writing in his mid-eighties. I was very impressed, I have to say. He's an unusual case, a very unusual writer. His last books were stronger than many younger writers' novels. *The Elephant's Journey* was a perfect work of art, and very funny.

STREITFELD: I see nothing in this room that smacks of our high-tech era.

LE GUIN: I have a website. I blog. I get email and send email. But I try and keep my distance. The internet just invites crap from people.

STREITFELD: You are the only writer I know who wrote a book about the street she lives on.

LE GUIN: It's called *Blue Moon Over Thurman Street*. It has wonderful photographs by Roger Dorband. The street didn't change for decades—it started at the docks, in industry, and moved through poverty and then small businesses to the working class and the middle class before petering out in hiking trails. It was a street that encapsulated America, or at least Portland. Thurman Street tied together the river with the hills, where the trees are.

STREITFELD: And then, suddenly, everything changed.

LE GUIN: Right after we wrote it in 1993 it was *boom!* The street went upscale. All the empty lots were filled in. They even changed the street down by the river to make it one-way, cutting off lower Thurman from upper Thurman. It reflected with incredible literalness the way America was no longer one place but two, one for the rich and the other for the poor. It was a split that didn't seem to bother anyone. That also reflected America.

STREITFELD: When did you first move here?

LE GUIN: In 1959. It's a mail-order house. Sears Roebuck sent the plans, and the local carpenter built it with local wood. The one next door is this house plus a whole other wing. This neighborhood was originally upper middle class, a development for business owners and such. By the time we got here it was very run down, lower middle class or upper working class. We were young. Charles was an assistant professor. We didn't have much money and were starting a family. It was a beautiful big house on a hill. We just waltzed in here and said "Oh yeah." You know what it cost us? $12,500. It's about a half a million now.

STREITFELD: Thurman Street is filled with places to while away an afternoon or maybe a lifetime. I had an excellent cup of coffee at the Clearing Café.

LE GUIN: I don't know it. It must be new. The Crackerjacks bar hangs on, the one constant. Charles is from Georgia, so going to a bar is not part of his culture, but we used to go into the Crackerjacks now and then. We don't drink much beer anymore. I don't know who goes there. Not the trendy people.

STREITFELD: You've received a lot of honors and awards over the years, and the pace has picked up recently, but there's a sense among your admirers that you still haven't gotten your due—that your influence and accomplishments are only beginning to be charted.

LE GUIN: I've had a big influence, yeah. But I published as a genre writer when genre was not literature. So what can you say? I didn't play by the literary rules at the time. I wrote what was not literature. I wrote genre. I paid the price. Don DeLillo, who comes off as literary without question, takes the award over me because I published in genre and he didn't. Also, he's a man and I'm a woman.

[That happened thirty years earlier, but clearly the wound was still fresh. In 1985 Le Guin published *Always Coming Home*, a story about people in California's Napa Valley who, she liked to say, "might be going to have lived a long, long time from now." It was her longest work of fiction and her most unconventional, using stories, original folktales, poetry, a glossary, dramatic works, illustrations, maps and mock histories to depict a society that might be a utopia. The book, released in a box with a cassette tape of music and songs that were an integral part of the story, did not sell well. It was too mainstream for science fiction, too much like science fiction for the mainstream. But it did become one of the three finalists for the National Book Award for fiction. DeLillo went home with the prize for *White Noise*, a tale of an airborne toxic event that borrowed certain motifs from science fiction. In early 2019, the Library of America plans to publish *Always Coming Home* as the fourth volume in its authoritative series of Le Guin's works, a vindication of her original hopes for the tale.]

STREITFELD: You were a pioneer.

LE GUIN: Remember, always: you're talking to a woman. And for a woman any literary award, honors, notice is an uphill job. And if she insists upon flouting convention and writing sci-fi and fantasy and indescribable stuff, well, you know how it's going to end up.

STREITFELD: Is the situation any better now?

LE GUIN: I have fits of—well, it isn't envy, because I don't want celebrity, not at all. And it isn't exactly jealousy. But sometimes my nose is out of joint when I see some kind of crappy writer getting all sorts of literary honors and I know I write better than he or she does. But all writers feel that way.

STREITFELD: In my experience, writers always want the opposite of what they have. If you sell ten million copies, you want to win the Nobel Prize. Win the Nobel Prize, and you want to sell ten million copies.

LE GUIN: That's human nature.

STREITFELD: Still, you have been much honored of late.

There is the 2014 National Book Foundation Medal for Distinguished Contribution to American Letters, and the Library of America is publishing your books.

LE GUIN: I don't think the honors have been overdone. I think I earned them. They are welcome and useful to me because they shore up my self-esteem, which seems to wobble as you get old. And particularly with the National Book Foundation speech, it was really nice to know that people listened.

STREITFELD: You presented a bleak vision in that speech, but said that artists could help us out of it: "Hard times are coming, when we'll be wanting the voices of writers who can see alternatives to how we live now." It went viral.

LE GUIN: I certainly didn't foresee Donald Trump. I was talking about longer-term hard times than that. For thirty years I've been saying, we are making the world uninhabitable, for God's sake. For forty years!

That, as of old, was the writer's job, maybe his primary job. To show us the futures we didn't want, and the futures we could have if we wanted. The key line in the speech, for me, was the one about, "We live in capitalism, its power seems inescapable—but then, so did the divine right of kings." We can change our lives.

STREITFELD: Did the speech come easily?

LE GUIN: It took months to write. It was implied to me that we should be short and I kept trying to make it shorter. They were trying to speed the ceremony up a bit because writers will just babble on.

STREITFELD: The Library of America is the Valhalla of publishing—your hero Hemingway, Edith Wharton, Henry James. Only a few contemporary writers have been honored while they were still alive—Eudora Welty and Saul Bellow among the novelists, John Ashbery and Bill Merwin among the poets. Oh, and Philip Roth.

LE GUIN: Curious company. [*Chuckles*]

STREITFELD: I could have guessed you were not a Roth fan.

LE GUIN: I kept trying to read him. I couldn't. Anyway, I didn't know when the library contacted me that the number of living writers they had enshrined was that low. What caught my attention was when they republished some Phil Dick, a dozen or so novels spread over three volumes. I thought, "Well, well, well. The old genre walls really are crumbling." But the distinction between the living and the dead didn't initially occur to me.

I was a French scholar, or thought I would be. So I knew the French series of classics, the Pléiade. I think of them as sacred. They were the entire canon of the great literature of the French—such beautiful books on that very, very thin India paper with the golden binding.

In this country, sets of an author's work were not such a big deal. I grew up with a set of Mark Twain in the house. My agent was a little iffy about dealing with the Library of America. "They don't pay beans." She was pretty scornful. I said, "Ginger, come on! Class! Kudos!" And she said, "Well, yeah, sure. But all the same, they don't pay beans." That's because most of the people they handle are dead. But I'm not in it for the money. I have to coax Ginger into some of the deals I make. She's a good agent. Her job is to make money. But I like a well-made book, and the Library of America volumes are well made. And the editing seems to be done with great care, line editing like no one does anymore.

STREITFELD: How did your first volume for the Library of America become the 1979 novel *Malafrena* and other stories from the place you call Orsinia? When most people think of Le Guin, they don't first think of fiction about an imaginary nineteenth-century country.

LE GUIN: I bullied them into doing Orsinia first. I didn't realize I was bullying them, but I was. They were very good-natured about it. They were going for the sci-fi, the science fiction, straight off and I kind of felt, okay, the Library of America is a literary series, and I've insisted for fifty years that science fiction properly done is literature. But it's not all I write and I'm tired of having always foregrounded "the sci-fi writer." No, I'm not a sci-fi writer. I'm a writer. I write novels, short stories, and poems, of various kinds. To just republish the same things that everyone republishes all the time, the old works, that I wrote way way back, does not interest me.

STREITFELD: You bend even the Library of America to your ways.

LE GUIN: What have I got to lose?

STREITFELD: You were this way fifty years ago.

LE GUIN: I really was. There's some innate arrogance here. I want to do it my way. People are always trying to pigeonhole me and push me off the literary scene, and to hell with it. [*Chuckles*] I won't be pushed.

STREITFELD: That even extends to the way you deal with publishers.

LE GUIN: So much writing about being a writer is about how you have to do it their way. I have never—or at least very, very seldom—made any deal for an unwritten work in my whole career. I write it and then sell it. That wasn't so unusual fifty years ago, but it is now. I don't promise work. People ask, will you write us a short story? I might, but I'm not signing any contract. No way do I contract for any unwritten work, ever. Way back my agent Virginia Kidd did it to me a couple of times and I gave her hell. I don't write to order. I write to private order, to internal orders. Most of my fellow authors want a deadline. I ask for deadlines on nonfiction. "When you want this?" But when it comes to the stuff that comes from inside me, the fiction and poetry, I demand an extraordinary and unusual amount of liberty.

STREITFELD: The readers of *Malafrena* and the Orsinia stories have always struggled to locate them, sometimes literally. Orsinia seems like Hungary, but you once suggested Czechoslovakia. Poland seemed possible too.

LE GUIN: They take place in an imaginary Central European country but within the framework of European history. It's confusing to people. What do you call the stories? It's not alternative history because it's just European history. There is no name for it. I do things like that. Parts of *Malafrena* go back decades, to the beginning of my career. I sold the first Orsinia story, "An die Musik," in 1960 to the *Western Humanities Review*. That same week I sold my first fantasy story, "April in Paris." I had two horses running. Fantasy paid better.

STREITFELD: There's a quote I love, from *Always Coming Home*: "A book is an act; it takes place in time, not just space. It is not information, but relation." With your books, they looked like one thing in the 1960s and '70s. They looked like—forgive me—escapist trash, bought off a paperback rack, never reviewed, disposed of after consuming. And now they'll be in those elegant, austere Library of America editions that are on acid-free paper that will last forever, or thereabouts. And yet they're the same stories.

LE GUIN: And yet they're the same stories. That's what matters to me . . .

[She leafed through some of the books I had brought along. The 1967 Ace paperback of *City of Illusions* showed shadowy figures and rocketships, with the cover line: "Was he a human meteor or a time-bomb from the stars?" On *Rocannon's World*, half of a 1966 Ace Double, a man holding a torch is riding a winged beast in outer space. The blurb: "Wherever he went, his super-science made him a legendary figure."]

LE GUIN: Those are actually pretty good covers compared to some I got. There was the awful *Wizard of Earthsea* paperback from Ace that showed the shadow leaping onto Ged's shoulders.

My books have risen above their Ace origins, their antecedents. They come from a nice working class family. I'm not remotely ashamed of their origins, but I am not captivated by them either the way some people are. Some people are fascinated by the pulps—there's something remote and glamorous in the whole idea of a twenty-five-cent book. I am in the middle of re-reading Michael Chabon's *The Amazing Adventures of Kavalier and Clay*. Michael is enthralled by the whole comic book thing. That is perfectly understandable and I enjoy his fascination, but my mind doesn't work that way. I am into content. Presentation? That is just something that has to be there.

STREITFELD: How do you feel about e-books these days? In

2008 you wrote for *Harper's Magazine* about the alleged decline of reading. It now seems prophetic about the reliability and durability of physical books: "If a book told you something when you were fifteen, it will tell it to you again when you're fifty, though you may understand it so differently that it seems you're reading a whole new book."

LE GUIN: When I started writing about e-books and print books, a lot of people were shouting "The book is dead, the book is dead, it's all going to be electronic." I got tired of it. What I was trying to say is that now we have two ways of publishing, and we're going to use them both. We had one, now we have two. How can that be bad? Creatures live longer if they can do things different ways. I think I've been fairly consistent on that. But the tone of my voice might have changed. I was going against a trendy notion. There's this joke I heard. You know what Gutenberg's second book was, after the Bible? It was a book about how the book was dead.

Personally, though, I hate to read on a screen. I don't have an e-reader.

STREITFELD: Speaking of Kindles, you've been a vocal critic of Amazon.

LE GUIN: Their wish to control is what scares me. What I want people to worry about is the extent this corporation controls what is published. Amazon sets the norm—if it's interested, the publisher increases the print run. If it's not, the print run goes down. Jeff Bezos has got all the guns on his side. I hate to put in war imagery here about everything being a battle, but I don't know any other way.

STREITFELD: Some writers grumble to me about Amazon, but they're reluctant to be public about it because they think it will hurt their careers. Others say they do not see an issue here at all.

LE GUIN: Amazon is extremely clever at making people love it, as if it were a nice uncle. I don't expect to win, but I still need to say what I think. When I am afraid to say what I think is when I will really be defeated. The only way they can defeat me is by silencing me. I might as well go out kicking.

STREITFELD: You and Phil Dick were the two great science fiction writers of the 1960s and '70s. You grew up a few miles from each other. You both went to Berkeley High. You graduated together, in 1947. You wrote in 1971 one of the best Phil Dick novels that Phil Dick never wrote, *The Lathe of Heaven*. You called him, in *The New Republic*, "our home-grown Borges." He said some complimentary things about you in public and some less than complimentary things in private. You tangled in the pages of fanzines over his depiction of women, and he credited you with his luminous creation of Angel Archer in his last novel, *The Transmigration of Timothy Archer*. She was his most complex female character. I suspect monographs will be written one day about your influence on each other—and yet you never met.

LE GUIN: He was self-isolated. He went through Berkeley High with no one knowing him. I was shy but my picture was in the yearbook. His was not. He would scare people off. He scared his wives off. He was a loner—very ambitious, very self-destructive.

STREITFELD: He scared you off. He wanted to come visit you at one of his many low points, in the early 1970s. He tried to reassure you that the rumors you had heard weren't true. "I swear I can conduct a civilized, rational conversation, without breaking anybody's favorite lamp," he wrote.

LE GUIN: I was terrified he would just show up. I had young children.

STREITFELD: You wrote about Dick in a 1974 letter to James Tiptree, Jr., "We are both scared to death of each other. Each of us is the other's Unconscious, I think." And then you added: "Geniuses do tend to be overwhelming, I guess, don't they?"

LE GUIN: What some consider a mystical breakthrough late in Phil's life looks to me more like a breakdown. Still, this was a remarkable mind. But his works don't wear as well as I hoped and thought they would.

STREITFELD: Oh no!

LE GUIN: I did an introduction to the Folio Society edition of *The Man in the High Castle*, and re-reading it I was struck by the clunkiness. Others that I liked a lot I now find hard going. I'm afraid to re-read *Galactic Pot-Healer*, my secret favorite. *Clans of the Alphane Moon*, which I was crazy about, now seems cruel. The way he handled women was pretty bad.

STREITFELD: There is a utility box on a street next to Berkeley High that devotes one side to you and another to Dick, the school's two most famous graduates.

LE GUIN: I've never heard of that. This is a huge school. They must have famous graduates other than us.

[When I got home, I sent her pictures. The utility box was not well kept up, and there was graffiti on it. On the third side was playwright Thornton Wilder. On the fourth side was a relatively recent graduate named Ariel Schrag, a cartoonist. Le Guin wrote back: "Wow. I gotta monument. It's hard to tell, but it looks like I gotta mustache, too. Fair enough. I never knew Thornton Wilder went to BHS! I've always liked his stuff. Live and learn."]

STREITFELD: I live near Berkeley, and you seem to haunt the place. Your father was a professor at Cal. A big building on campus is named after him. The family ranch in Napa, which you've returned to every year, is not far away. Parnassus Press, the original publisher of *A Wizard of Earthsea*, was based in Berkeley.

LE GUIN: I grew up on a house on a hill in Berkeley, at 1325 Arch Street. It was then a lower-middle class neighborhood. Now it's very expensive, near the Gourmet Ghetto and Chez Panisse. I wrote an essay about the house, "Living in a Work of Art," about how it was designed by Bernard Maybeck in 1907 and was a wonderful if sometimes scary place for a child. The floors creaked long after you walked on them. The house was a complex space, even a moral space, and had an influence on me I can only begin to understand. My family owned it for fifty-four years, until my mother's death in 1979.

I sort of do and don't belong in the Bay Area. I grew up there but left at seventeen and never lived there full-time again. I just visited, and stayed there in summers with my family. I had friends and relatives all over the place for a while. But I was never ever part of the California literary scene—the Beats and so on. San Francisco has had quite the glory days but I've never felt so unwelcome in any bookstore as City Lights. Oh, they were so snotty.

STREITFELD: They were? They carry more of your books than anyone else in the Bay Area.

LE GUIN: This was twenty years ago, thirty years ago. They were very male-oriented. Come on. I've got nothing against City Lights. They're great and I'm glad they're there and I'm glad they're keeping going, but it never was much of a pleasure to go into in the old days. It's a kind of underground snobbishness. They make you feel like a middle-aged housewife, because they're so liberated and San Francisco is male.

Well, what do you do when you actually are a middle-aged housewife? The Beats weren't good to women, with their addiction scene.

STREITFELD: I never think of you as contemporary with the Beats, but you were. Jack Kerouac was only seven years older than you, Allen Ginsberg barely three. You had the last laugh on the Beats. You're still alive.

LE GUIN: Being a housewife and not being an addict prepares you for being eighty in ways that a life of wild living does not. The Beats died young, many of them. The great survivor is Gary Snyder. He was the one who didn't dope.

STREITFELD: Someone needs to do a monograph on Parnassus Press, publisher of *A Wizard of Earthsea* and much more. Very little is known about them.

LE GUIN: They were called Parnassus because they started in the late 1950s on a street named Parnassus. It was just Herman Schein and his wife, Ruth Robbins. They published my mother's book, *Ishi: The Last of His Tribe*, in 1964. That's how they found out about me. Herman was cranky, difficult. He asked me if I would write a fantasy for teenagers. I said I could never do that. Then it was, "Oh wow, I got this idea." Robbins, who did the illustrations, was a darling. She, and Herman, had no difficulty in understanding that the hero Ged is not a white man. Herman died rather young, and Ruth sold the press to Houghton Mifflin. They never got the credit they deserved as a children's press. They did beautiful books.

STREITFELD: *A Wizard of Earthsea* seems steeped in the Bay Area—the hills, the rain, the fog, the sense of never being far from the ocean. There's a line I love in "Living in a Work of Art" about "the extraordinary light of the Bay Area, which combines inland sunshine with sea-reflected radiance." I always imagine Earthsea to be like that.

LE GUIN: Havnor, the capital of Earthsea, was modeled on San Francisco. I could see it from my bedroom in Berkeley, a long way away. The world was bigger then. This was before the Bay Bridge, before the Golden Gate. To get to San Francisco, you took a ferry. It was an expedition, not a commute.

STREITFELD: You once did a script of *Earthsea*, with the legendary English director Michael Powell. That was back in the early 1980s, I think.

LE GUIN: That script is kind of a miracle. He got in touch, said he liked the books. We put the first two books—*Wizard* and *The Tombs of Atuan*—together. It moves with the stately Powell pace. The story is very old fashioned, an English school story. You could have made a movie out of it then. I don't think it would work now. It would be childish.

STREITFELD: There is a lot of debate about the right age for children to read *Wizard*.

LE GUIN: The Parnassus first edition had on it "11 up." They took that off very soon, because it was just about that point that the publishers were inventing the "young adult." YA became a recognized publishing genre and Herman Schein realized that the way to define this book is YA, not "11 up." But I kind of like "11 up." A lot of nine-year-olds read *A Wizard of Earthsea*. I don't think I would have understood it at nine but kids are very sophisticated now. Adult relationships are being talked about in the book—that can be really boring to a kid. But I don't know.

STREITFELD: There's a new *Earthsea* omnibus of the first four books that was just published by Puffin in England. It has supplementary material in the back that seems geared to very young readers.

LE GUIN: Young or stupid. I had a discussion about this with my editor at Puffin. She said, "The schools want it." If that's true, English schools are not what they used to be. But you can't argue with an editor that says schools want it. I hate all back matter—"Questions for your book group" and so on. I just won't look at it.

STREITFELD: The esteemed critic John Clute said every science fiction novel is secretly about the year it is written, and reflects what the writer was thinking and the cultural attitudes of the time.

LE GUIN: Inevitably!

STREITFELD: Would *Wizard* be fundamentally different if it had been written ten years later?

LE GUIN: Clute was talking about science fiction. This is fantasy. Fantasy draws on a much older, deeper well for its models, inspiration, style, everything. Science fiction is time-bound in a way that fantasy can be but does not need to be. But I can never answer questions like that. Ten years later I was a different person, so of course I would have written a different novel.

STREITFELD: You began by writing firmly within the male power hierarchy. In *Wizard*, women take a secondary role. There are sayings in *Earthsea* about "weak as woman's magic" and "wicked as woman's magic." The wizard school on Roke does not admit girls. Wizards are celibate.

LE GUIN: I was comfortably writing within that tradition in the 1960s, and then I was uncomfortable writing within it. *Earthsea* certainly would have been different if I started it ten years later. I had to turn around in the fourth volume, *Tehanu*, and untie it, untie the whole *Earthsea* from the male-centered, happily hierarchical, top-down world of the old fantasies. In coming back to *Earthsea* after seventeen years, what was interesting and reassuring to me was the realization that it wasn't any longer going to be about heroes in a happily male-dominated world, with no sex for the wizards. I didn't want to do that anymore, I couldn't do it anymore. It wasn't true anymore. And yet it was still *Earthsea*. I didn't have to change anything, I just had to explain it. It was quite an education for me, actually, writing those last few books—the fourth, fifth and sixth. Now it's done. I could go on and do sequels about other people in Earthsea but no. A story has an arc. You don't want to go on after the end of *King Lear*.

STREITFELD: I interviewed you in 1990 when *Tehanu* came out. You said, "Finally the story is done."

LE GUIN: I was wrong. I've been wrong about a lot of things about *Earthsea*. But now I believe I'm right.*

STREITFELD: You wrote *Lavinia* after you did the later *Earthsea* books. It was a novel about a character in the Aeneid, that translates the latter part of the epic, that revisions it, that is an explicit dialogue with its author, Virgil, as well as a tribute to him. As so often with your work, people had a hard time categorizing it.

LE GUIN: *Lavinia* doesn't fit, just like Orsinia doesn't fit. It's not science fiction, not fantasy, not realism. Why the hell does it have to fit a label? Labels—that's how you sell. And that's how you shelve at the library. It can be helpful but it is limiting.

The thing to do is get away from these late-twentieth-century attitudes. What does Borges write? You can only call it Borgesian. Kafka is Kafkaesque. There is no label for what

---

* She wasn't, quite. A last Earthsea story, "Firelight"—a moving account of Ged's dying, with Tenar by his side—appeared in the Summer 2018 issue of *The Paris Review*, six months after Le Guin's own death.

Calvino does. Calvinistic? It's just what Calvino does. What you really want is to be your own label.

STREITFELD: You recently said you've stopped writing fiction.

LE GUIN: I didn't say I stopped. I said, "The fiction isn't coming." It's never been a matter of "I will write" or "I won't write." I'm not getting short stories. I haven't gotten a story now for quite a while. "Elementals" was in *Tin House* in 2012, and then they published "The Jar of Water" in 2014 after the *New Yorker* sat on it forever and then didn't take it, which was very un-*New Yorker*–like. That's probably my last written, last published story.

STREITFELD: *Lavinia* in 2008 was your last novel.

LE GUIN: There just wasn't another novel lurking somewhere at the back of my consciousness. It's a very strange feeling, like having a well and the well goes dry. It's a disappointment and a letdown, it's work I loved doing. I know I can do it, so there's a feeling of waste. I have my profession, my art. I'm good at it. It's a pity I can't use it on what I love to use it on most, which is fiction. But I've got to have a story that picks me up and carries me. If it ain't there it ain't there. What is the use sitting around and whining about writer's block? It's not writer's block. I'm just written out. I'm glad I still can write poetry. I started with that and can continue with it now. That is both a lifelong need and a solace. If that gives out, I will be frustrated.

PART II

STREITFELD: You once clarified your political stance by saying, "I am not a progressive. I think the idea of progress an invidious and generally harmful mistake. I am interested in change, which is an entirely different matter." Why is the idea of progress harmful? Surely in the great sweep of time, there has been progress on social issues because people have an idea or even an ideal of it.

LE GUIN: I didn't say progress was harmful, I said the idea of progress was generally harmful. I was thinking more as a Darwinist than in terms of social issues. I was thinking about the idea of evolution as an ascending staircase with amoebas at the bottom and Man at the top or near the top, maybe with some angels above him. And I was thinking of the idea of history as ascending infallibly to the better—which, it seems to me, is how the nineteenth and twentieth centuries tended to use the word "progress." We leave behind us the Dark Ages of ignorance, the primitive ages without steam engines, without airplanes/nuclear power/computers/whatever is next. Progress discards the old, leads ever to the new, the better, the faster, the bigger, etc. You see my problem with it? It just isn't true.

STREITFELD: How does evolution fit in?

LE GUIN: Evolution is a wonderful process of change—of differentiation and diversification and complication, endless and splendid; but I can't say that any of its products is "better than" or "superior to" any other in general terms. Only in specific ways. Rats are more intelligent and more adaptable than koala bears, and those two superiorities will keep rats going while the koalas die out. On the other hand, if there were nothing around to eat but eucalyptus, the rats would be gone in no time and the koalas would thrive. Humans can do all kinds of stuff bacteria can't do, but if I had to bet on really long-term global survival, my money would go to the bacteria.

STREITFELD: In the Library of America's edition of Orsinia, you quote from a 1975 journal when you were finishing up the novel that you began in the 1950s, *Malafrena*. You realized that in many ways it was spiritually and thematically similar to the novel you had just finished, *The Dispossessed*. You wrote, "not only the person and the situation are similar but the *words*: —True pilgrimage consists in coming home—True journey is return—and so on. I have not a *few* ideas: I have ONE idea."

LE GUIN: [*Laughs*] People will take it literally, and they will quote it as the gospel truth, but what the hell—you just can't write for stupid people. I beat up myself considerably about putting that section of a private diary in print. I've never done anything really like that before. I just kind of thought, "Oh, what the hell." I wrote it and reading it decades later said, "Yeah, okay, there's some truth in that, and what have I to risk?"

STREITFELD: The idea turns up everywhere in your work. You wrote a poem called "GPS" which ends:

There are two places: home, away. I lack
A map that shows me anywhere but those.

LE GUIN: Another major version of that idea is *Always Coming Home*. It's even in the title. That's one of my most neglected and most central books. You want to understand how my mind works, go there. In the novel within the book, Stone Telling starts in the valley, goes to a different valley and comes back. There's this whole difference between the circle and the spiral. We say the Earth has a circular orbit around the Sun, but of course it doesn't. The sun moves too. You never come back to the same place, you just come back to the same point on the spiral. That image is very deep in my thinking. You can't come home again and you can never step in the same river again. I quote that over and over again.

STREITFELD: Is this *the* central fantasy notion? It's certainly in many fairy tales and ghost stories. I'm not sure how many of your peers are preoccupied by it.

LE GUIN: I recognize it in Borges. We're very different writers, but he uses that notion too. Saramago—and Borges too, for that matter—is fascinated by the idea of doubles. I don't go there.

Is going home a central fantasy notion? I think that would be a very interesting question to explore. Certainly it's a central idea of *The Lord of the Rings*. But of fantasy? It may be *a* central idea, one of them. The first great fantasy is *The Odyssey*. And what does Odysseus do? He comes home.

Homecoming may not be such an easy visit, after all. The world is changing. It is a spiral. That is kind of the point.

STREITFELD: The idea has less appeal in science fiction. The central SF idea, as molded in the 1940s, is, "We're going to Mars, to another galaxy. We're out of here and we ain't coming back."

LE GUIN: Outer space was an extension of the frontier—"We're going to California in 1849. We're gone." I just discovered, though, that some people went back and forth, including my own family. My great grandfather, James Johnston, was a '49er. He went out on the immigrant trail the first year of the Gold Rush, spent quite a while in California, ranched a while in Steens Mountain in Oregon—why, I can't imagine—and then went back on the immigrant trail to Missouri. He ended up in Wyoming. There were a lot of people who did something like that. You always hear about the westward movement. You don't hear about the backwash. Once you get to the frontier and there is no more frontier, what do you do? Well, you find a new frontier. That was talked about a lot in the 1940s, the 1950s. What is the new frontier? It's the moon, outer space. We must have a new frontier, we must go forward! It fits in with capitalism, after all.

STREITFELD: In 1974, you published an essay, "Why Are Americans Afraid of Dragons?" You wrote, "I think a great many American men have been taught to repress their imaginations, to reject it as something childish or effeminate, unprofitable, and probably sinful." Fantasy was kept in the nursery or with the outcasts.

LE GUIN: Americans are no longer afraid of dragons, I think it's fair to say. [*Laughs*] What's that old saying, Be careful of what you wish for? The panic is dying. We're going back to the mixture as it was before in earlier generations, when realism and fantasy mixed in all sorts of different ways.

STREITFELD: We're inundated with fantasy now.

LE GUIN: But much of it is derivative; you can mash a lot of orcs and unicorns and intergalactic wars together without actually imagining anything. One of the troubles with our culture is we do not respect and train the imagination. It needs exercise. It needs practice. You can't tell a story unless you've listened to a lot of stories and then learned how to do it.

STREITFELD: When the new *Ghostbusters* movie came out, and it had an all-female cast, the culture trembled. There were riots in the street, almost. Is fantasy now infantilizing us?

LE GUIN: I was talking about the genrification of fantasy literature. When you get into the whole pop-culture side of things, I don't know what goes on there. The retreat into childishness is not a special characteristic of fantasy, but it can be a characteristic of almost anything.

STREITFELD: I stand corrected.

LE GUIN: To genrify is necessary. There are different genres. What is wrong is to rank them as higher or lower, to make a hierarchy based only on genre, not the quality of the writing. That is my whole argument and it goes no further. So don't try to extend it into this world.

STREITFELD: You noted the tendency in American culture to leave the unbridled imagination to kids, who will grow out of it to become good businessmen or good politicians. Has that changed?

LE GUIN: Maybe it's changed some.

STREITFELD: The battle has been won?

LE GUIN: Can we get away from the battle metaphor, and from winning and losing? Things have changed and maybe they've changed in that perspective, and in a good direction. You talk about winning and losing. I see it as, you make a gain here and then discover you lost something there.

STREITFELD: Okay.

LE GUIN: The place where the unbridled—not a word I'd use—imagination worries me is when it becomes part of nonfiction. You're allowed to lie in a memoir now. In fact, sometimes you're encouraged. I'm not a curmudgeon, I'm just a scientist's daughter. I really like facts. I have a huge re-spect for them. The indifference toward factuality that is en-couraged in a lot of nonfiction—it worries me when people put living people into a novel. Even when you put in rather recently dead people, it always seems you're taking a terrific risk. There's a kind of insolence about it, a kind of coloniza-tion of that person by you, the author. Is that right, is that fair? And then we get these biographers where they are sort of making it up as they go along. I don't want to read that. I always think, what is it, a novel, a biography, what is it?

It's funny. As a novelist, my requirements for a non-fiction book are different than for many nonfiction writers. The difference between fiction and nonfiction to me is pretty absolute. Either you're making it up or trying to figure out what happened and say it as well as you can. Your own bi-ases will get in the way and nobody can be perfectly factual, but you try. The main thing is trying. It seems to me a lot of people have given up trying, and the reviewers give them their blessing. But we have to be factual. Ask any scientist.

STREITFELD: Reality is so murky . . .

LE GUIN: Of course. So don't make it murkier.

STREITFELD: History used to be about white men.

LE GUIN: That wasn't wrong for previous generations. It is for this society. Times change.

I can't make moral judgments about what was wrong

and right a hundred or two hundred years ago. I don't live in that world. We have so much trouble reading history without colonizing it, without asking how could you possibly be in favor of slavery or whatever. As if they had the ideas in their head to think the way we do. It's so unfair.

There's a sort of absolutism today. You do one bad thing and you're a bad person. That's just childish. There's a lot of childishness around.

STREITFELD: The culture is getting more intolerant?

LE GUIN: There's a tendency that way.

STREITFELD: But in some ways, there's greater acceptance too. We've talked about how your work has made the transition from sci-fi to lit.

LE GUIN: I existed as an Ace double, half of a back-to-back paperback. We got somewhere. But then you look around and find out it really is the same place after all. Remember the spiral? That's how I see it. It's the same. America's still America. [*Laughs*]

People are seeing the stories differently, with different eyes. That's good, I'm happy. I'm delighted. It never was a battle to me exactly, and winning and losing are not the terms I would choose to talk in. It was a change I wanted to see happen, and in its own way and its own time it has happened and is happening.

STREITFELD: I'm reading your mother's book about your father, *Alfred Kroeber: A Personal Configuration*. He died in 1960. Around the time the book was published, in 1970, your mother remarried, to a much younger man.

LE GUIN: John Quinn. I had it in my head that he was thirty and she was seventy-two but I'm not good with figures. He was a lot younger. Her ten years with him, up to the last year, which was illness and other trouble, she had a terrific time. He just spoiled her rotten. He did it with a certain class. She had a good time.

STREITFELD: Have you ever been tempted to write more about your parents?

LE GUIN: Oh my Lord, it's impossible. They're just beyond me. She was . . . oh man. She was such a kind sweet mother. Men just ate out of her hand. Whatever "it" is she had "it." "It" with a capital "I."

STREITFELD: Since you've from time to time given me child-raising advice, I want you to know I took Lily, my eight-year-old, to see a production of *Snow White*. After it was over, all the kids lined up to have their picture taken with Snow White. Lily was the only one who wanted her picture taken with the Evil Queen.

LE GUIN: My eldest daughter took up the cello at age eight, and went on to become a cellist. Years later I said, "Elizabeth, how did you know to pick the cello?" And she said, "Oh it's just that everyone else was doing the violin."

Raising daughters is very interesting. My first daughter has always been just a good kid. My second daughter—oh my God. [*Laughs*] Is Lily a good reader?

STREITFELD: Yes. She takes books *to* the bookstore. If she can't find anything there, she'll have something to read on the way home. But she's at an age where things in books really scare her.

LE GUIN: She may not get over that. I never did. I'll stop reading because either I'm existentially terrified or it's just too scary.

STREITFELD: Maybe you're lucky you can still respond so intensely.

LE GUIN: I get sent a lot of books to blurb. I look at them. And so many have a lot of high tension, a lot of suspense. I'll get really scared, and then it will turn out to be the first book of a series. To hell with it. I don't respond well to suspense. I hate it. I'll look at the end of the story when I'm still at the beginning.

STREITFELD: Speaking of children, between 1966 and 1974, you raised three children and wrote a series of masterpieces. Much of the work in your second and third Library of America volumes was done in a short span of time—a few years during the late 1960s and early '70s. Did you feel at the time your brain was on fire?

LE GUIN: I worked just as hard before that and just as hard after. Why those years? That's not all my significant work. There's pretty good stuff after.

STREITFELD: But later your children were older. You had more time to write.

LE GUIN: I had a child under five at home for how many years? Probably seven or eight. No. 3 came along slightly un-expectedly, about the time No. 2 was beginning to go off to kindergarten. So all of a sudden I had a baby again, which was unexpected but profitable. I could not possibly have done it if Charles had not been a full-time parent. Over and over I've said it—two people can do three jobs but one person cannot do two. Well, sometimes they do, but it's a killer.

STREITFELD: How did you manage?

LE GUIN: I don't want to be Pollyannish but the fact is both jobs were very rewarding. They were *immediately* rewarding. I enjoy writing and I enjoyed the kids.

STREITFELD: You once said that having kids doesn't make the writing easier but it makes it better.

LE GUIN: When I discovered I was pregnant the third time I went through a bad patch. I thought, "We didn't really mean to do this thing. How are we going to do it all over again?" Pregnancy can be pretty devouring. But it was an easy preg-nancy, a great baby, and we were really really glad we did.

STREITFELD: The kids sometimes inspired stories. Caroline, age three, came to you with a small wooden box and asked you to guess what was inside. As I recall, you guessed caterpillars and elephants, but she opened the box a tiny bit, allowing you to peek inside, and said: "Darkness." That resulted in the story "Darkness Box."

LE GUIN: That was a direct influence, which is kind of rare. Usually it was more general. There was all this vitality in the house. I was lucky because I was healthy and the kids were healthy. That makes such a difference. But it didn't seem remarkable. I was of a generation when women were expected to—did expect to—have kids.

STREITFELD: Tillie Olsen, the author of *Tell Me a Riddle*, said that the need to earn money to support her family destroyed her as an artist. She's remembered for that assertion now as much as she is for her stories.

LE GUIN: Tillie was the generation before mine. She was also a much more fierce kind of feminist than I was. She made me rather uncomfortable. But the real difference between us was that Tillie didn't have any money. She had nine-to-five jobs or whatever she could get. That is a huge difference. I had friends in that position. It was particularly hard if the marriage was broken up. If they didn't have a husband pulling in some income, they tried very hard to keep doing their art, but they had to earn money. And so they had to make a choice I never really had to make.

STREITFELD: When did you write?

LE GUIN: After the kids were put to bed, or left in their room with a book. My kids went to bed much earlier than most kids do now. I was appalled to learn my grand-children were staying up to 11:00 p.m. That would have driven me up the wall. We got them down by old-fashioned hours—8:00 p.m., 9:00 p.m. I would go up to the attic, and have nine to midnight. If I was tired it was a little tough. But I was kind of gung ho to do it. I like to write. It's exciting.

STREITFELD: Writing came easily to you.

LE GUIN: Yes, I had ideas.

STREITFELD: You didn't try before bedtime?

LE GUIN: So long as I was in charge of the kids, that was that. It was full time. Sometimes Charles would be in charge, or they'd be out at music lessons. But I'm not very good at seiz-ing broken bits.

STREITFELD: And when you started, you worked efficiently?

LE GUIN: Depends on the book. Sometimes I just sat there for two hours.

STREITFELD: You put in a plug for Elizabeth Gaskell recently.

LE GUIN: *North and South* is outstanding. *Mary Barton* makes me cry every damn time.

Speaking of writers, you know who floats my literary agency? Ayn Rand. I couldn't read Hermann Hesse. He was boring but not as boring as Ayn Rand. I read *The Fountainhead* when I was twenty. About as loathsome a book as I've ever read.

STREITFELD: You have remained on good terms with Harlan Ellison.

LE GUIN: He was kind of adorable. Okay, not in a physical sense. But you would forgive the bastard anything. I've forgiven him a dozen times. Things I would not forgive anybody else. Because what the hell. It's just Harlan. He was so funny. And so much . . . I need Jewish words here.

STREITFELD: I have a lot of complex feelings about Harlan. All the bragging, the aggression, the time wasted in feuds . . .

LE GUIN: I never met a man who didn't have complex feelings about him. And most women too. I have complicated feelings too. He's a bastard. He did stupid dirty things to me. But they didn't amount to anything. [*Laughs*] Dastardly plots that didn't work out. Besides, he was a lot of fun to be with.

STREITFELD: Neil Gaiman is in some ways the star fantasy writer of the era.

LE GUIN: His fans are devoted. He works in many fields. All my contact with him has been good. He's truly generous. He's been very generous to me. [*Laughs*] I just wish I liked his writing more.

STREITFELD: You're now a member of the American Academy of Arts and Letters.

LE GUIN: I almost wasn't. It's so embarrassing. Either the letter got lost in the mail or I tossed it thinking it was junk, I don't know which, but in either case I never got the invitation. They waited and waited and waited and finally got in touch with my agent, who immediately got in touch with me. I wrote to them and said, "I wasn't pulling a Dylan." But they must have wondered.

STREITFELD: It's another honor, a significant one.

LE GUIN: To paraphrase Mary Wollstonecraft's line about the vindication of the rights of women, it's a vindication of the rights of science fiction. It makes it a lot harder for the diehards and holdouts to say, "Genre isn't literature."

STREITFELD: Do they still say that?

LE GUIN: You'd be surprised. In academe, there are still diehards. Once a critic takes a position, he never changes it.

STREITFELD: For all my devotion to your work, the vast

academic literature about it always seemed tough sledding.

LE GUIN: Well, they're academics. There was one book that really took me by surprise and gave me great pleasure. It was called *The New Utopian Politics of Ursula K. Le Guin's "The Dispossessed."* It came out in 2005 and practically everything in it was readable. That's very rare.

STREITFELD: Right after Trump's election, you came up with a new model of resistance that elevates not the warrior but water: "The flow of a river is a model for me of courage that can keep me going—carry me through the bad places, the bad times. A courage that is compliant by choice and uses force only when compelled."

LE GUIN: It's rooted firmly in Lao Tzu and the *Tao Te Ching*. He goes very deep in me, back to my teenage years. I've found him a helpful thinker. I did my own translation a few years back.

STREITFELD: There are traces of Lao Tzu in *Tehanu*, but it's not explicit.

LE GUIN: Most of my real work was fictional, where you don't express things like that directly. You build it in. Like in *The Lathe of Heaven*. George, the hero, is kind of watery. He goes with the flow, as they used to say. I was dubious about publishing that piece about water as a blog entry. It was so direct, and sounded like I was trying to be some sort of guru.

STREITFELD: You *are* direct.

LE GUIN: I like to hide it in fiction.

STREITFELD: For a year or two, you thought you would never write fiction again.

LE GUIN: But then I suddenly went and wrote a little story called "Calx" for *Catamaran*, and then a long story called "Pity and Shame." I should have remembered what all good SF writers know: prediction is not our game.

STREITFELD: Are you following the Me Too movement, as women assert themselves on social media after years of harassment?

LE GUIN: I don't follow things on social media, and I don't have very much faith in their endurance. Everybody explodes, get it out of their systems, and then they let it drop again.

STREITFELD: Maybe, although careers are definitely being affected here. Can we ever watch *House of Cards*, with its disgraced star, Kevin Spacey, again?

LE GUIN: If you start saying that about actors, you can't go to the theater.

STREITFELD: A couple of producers announced they were going to do a show, an alternate history of the Confederacy where the South won. There was an outpouring of rage against it. The very idea was offensive.

LE GUIN: That's political correctness gone mad, to ban a show that hasn't even been made. This is why I never write contemporary fiction. I would get raked over the coals by every politically correct anti-racist. I was able to populate Earthsea with brown and black people fifty years ago but it was fantasy and so no one took it seriously. That is why they could keep publishing science fiction in the Soviet Union that was critical of the regime. It's exactly the same thing. I would never get away with that today.

STREITFELD: I don't see the books you and Charles were reading last night. Usually they're on the tables here.

LE GUIN: He's now reading the *Oxford Book of English Verse* to me. I'm reading Brontë's *Shirley* to him. It's a good book, much better than I realized. I wasn't feeling so hot, so we had the reading upstairs, with a little whiskey. I'm still recovering from my birthday. It was very nice. It kind of went on for a week. My daughter came up from Los Angeles, and I got to see her. It's a serious age, eighty-eight. If you turn the numbers on their side, it's two infinities on top of each other.

URSULA KROEBER LE GUIN (1929-2018) was born in Berkeley and lived in Portland, Oregon. She published more than twenty novels, eleven volumes of short stories, six collections of essays, twelve books for children, six volumes of poetry, and four of translation. Among the many honors her writing received were a National Book Award, five Hugo Awards, five Nebula Awards, SFWA's Damon Wright Memorial Grand Master Award, the Kafka Award, a Pushcart Prize, the Harold D. Vursell Memorial Award of the American Academy of Arts and Letters, the *Los Angeles Times*'s Robert Kirsch Award, the PEN/Malamud Award, the Margaret A. Edwards Award, and in 2014 the National Book Foundation Medal for Distinguished Contribution to American Letters.

10 POINT 5 was a quarterly magazine of the arts in Eugene, Oregon. Its name came from the number of cycles per second that is the median alpha wave frequency of the human brain. The magazine published seven issues between early 1976 to summer 1978.

GEORGE WICKES and **LOUISE WESTLING** are retired University of Oregon English professors. Westling is the author of *The Green Breast of the New World*. Wickes wrote *Americans in Paris* and edited three collections of Henry Miller's letters.

NORA GALLAGHER writes memoir and fiction. She's the author recently of the memoir *Moonlight Sonata at Mayo Clinic* and the novel *Changing Light*.

DOROTHY GILBERT was a programmer and interviewer at radio station KPFA in Berkeley for ten years in the 1970s and 1980s. She was for many years on the staff of PEN America and has taught English at UC Berkeley. She has published two award-winning translations from Old French, poems in numerous journals, and science fiction.

NICK GEVERS is a critic and editor specializing in science fiction and fantasy. He has published hundreds of book reviews and scores of author interviews, and edited many anthologies, including the Shirley Jackson Award–winning *Ghosts by Gaslight* (with Jack Dann). He lives in Cape Town, South Africa.

BRIDGET HUBER is a journalist and researcher based in France. Her work has been published or broadcast by Public Radio International, *The Lancet*, *The New York Times*, *Mother Jones*, *California Sunday Magazine*, and National Public Radio, among others.

DAVID STREITFELD is the editor of *The Last Interview* books on Gabriel Garcia Marquez, J. D. Salinger, Philip K. Dick, Hunter Thompson, and, in its expanded form, David Foster Wallace. All were published by Melville House. He is a reporter for *The New York Times*, where in 2013 he was part of the team awarded the Pulitzer Prize for Explanatory Reporting. He lives in the San Francisco Bay Area with his family and too many books.

THE LAST INTERVIEW SERIES

**KURT VONNEGUT:
THE LAST INTERVIEW**

$15.95 / $17.95 CAN

978-1-61219-090-7
ebook: 978-1-61219-091-4

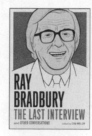

**RAY BRADBURY:
THE LAST INTERVIEW**

$15.95 / $15.95 CAN

978-1-61219-421-9
ebook: 978-1-61219-422-6

**JACQUES DERRIDA:
THE LAST INTERVIEW:
LEARNING TO LIVE
FINALLY**

$15.95 / $17.95 CAN

978-1-61219-094-5
ebook: 978-1-61219-032-7

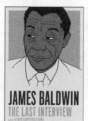

**JAMES BALDWIN:
THE LAST INTERVIEW**

$15.95 / $15.95 CAN

978-1-61219-400-4
ebook: 978-1-61219-401-1

**ROBERTO BOLAÑO:
THE LAST INTERVIEW**

$15.95 / $17.95 CAN

978-1-61219-095-2
ebook: 978-1-61219-033-4

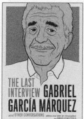

**GABRIEL GÁRCIA
MÁRQUEZ: THE LAST
INTERVIEW**

$15.95 / $15.95 CAN

978-1-61219-480-6
ebook: 978-1-61219-481-3

**JORGE LUIS BORGES:
THE LAST INTERVIEW**

$15.95 / $17.95 CAN

978-1-61219-204-8
ebook: 978-1-61219-205-5

**LOU REED: THE LAST
INTERVIEW**

$15.95 / $15.95 CAN

978-1-61219-478-3
ebook: 978-1-61219-479-0

**HANNAH ARENDT:
THE LAST INTERVIEW**

$15.95 / $15.95 CAN

978-1-61219-311-3
ebook: 978-1-61219-312-0

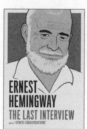

**ERNEST HEMINGWAY:
THE LAST INTERVIEW**

$15.95 / $20.95 CAN

978-1-61219-522-3
ebook: 978-1-61219-523-0

THE LAST INTERVIEW SERIES

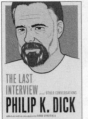

PHILIP K. DICK: THE LAST INTERVIEW

$15.95 / $20.95 CAN

978-1-61219-526-1
ebook: 978-1-61219-527-8

MARTIN LUTHER KING, JR.: THE LAST INTERVIEW

$15.99 / $21.99 CAN

978-1-61219-616-9
ebook: 978-1-61219-617-6

NORA EPHRON: THE LAST INTERVIEW

$15.95 / $20.95 CAN

978-1-61219-524-7
ebook: 978-1-61219-525-4

CHRISTOPHER HITCHENS: THE LAST INTERVIEW

$15.99 / $20.99 CAN

978-1-61219-672-5
ebook: 978-1-61219-673-2

JANE JACOBS: THE LAST INTERVIEW

$15.95 / $20.95 CAN

978-1-61219-534-6
ebook: 978-1-61219-535-3

HUNTER S. THOMPSON: THE LAST INTERVIEW

$15.99 / $20.99 CAN

978-1-61219-693-0
ebook: 978-1-61219-694-7

DAVID BOWIE: THE LAST INTERVIEW

$16.99 / $22.99 CAN

978-1-61219-575-9
ebook: 978-1-61219-576-6

DAVID FOSTER WALLACE: THE LAST INTERVIEW

$16.99 / 21.99 CAN

978-1-61219-741-8
ebook: 978-1-61219-742-5